The Darkest Captive

Also from Gena Showalter

The Darkest Captive

A Lords of the Underworld Novella

By Gena Showalter

1001 Dark Nights

EVIL EYE
CONCEPTS

The Darkest Captive
A Lords of the Underworld Novella
By Gena Showalter

1001 Dark Nights
Copyright 2018 Gena Showalter
ISBN: 978-1-948050-03-6

Foreword: Copyright 2014 M. J. Rose
Published by Evil Eye Concepts, Incorporated

Acknowledgments from the Author

To Liz Berry, MJ Rose and Jillian Stein. I love and adore you guys, and I'm so blessed to work with you. Sorry, girls, but you are just stuck with me for life.

And to Jill Monroe for never being afraid to tell me "You did this wrong."

Sign up for the 1001 Dark Nights Newsletter
and be entered to win a Tiffany Key necklace.

There's a contest every month!

Go to www.1001DarkNights.com to subscribe.

As a bonus, all subscribers will receive a free copy of
Discovery Bundle Three
Featuring stories by
Sidney Bristol, Darcy Burke, T. Gephart
Stacey Kennedy, Adriana Locke
JB Salsbury, and Erika Wilde

One Thousand and One Dark Nights

Once upon a time, in the future...

*I was a student fascinated with stories and learning.
I studied philosophy, poetry, history, the occult, and
the art and science of love and magic. I had a vast
library at my father's home and collected thousands
of volumes of fantastic tales.*

*I learned all about ancient races and bygone
times. About myths and legends and dreams of all
people through the millennium. And the more I read
the stronger my imagination grew until I discovered
that I was able to travel into the stories... to actually
become part of them.*

*I wish I could say that I listened to my teacher
and respected my gift, as I ought to have. If I had, I
would not be telling you this tale now.
But I was foolhardy and confused, showing off
with bravery.*

*One afternoon, curious about the myth of the
Arabian Nights, I traveled back to ancient Persia to
see for myself if it was true that every day Shahryar
(Persian: شهريار, "king") married a new virgin, and then
sent yesterday's wife to be beheaded. It was written
and I had read, that by the time he met Scheherazade,
the vizier's daughter, he'd killed one thousand
women.*

Something went wrong with my efforts. I arrived in the midst of the story and somehow exchanged places with Scheherazade – a phenomena that had never occurred before and that still to this day, I cannot explain.

Now I am trapped in that ancient past. I have taken on Scheherazade's life and the only way I can protect myself and stay alive is to do what she did to protect herself and stay alive.

Every night the King calls for me and listens as I spin tales. And when the evening ends and dawn breaks, I stop at a point that leaves him breathless and yearning for more. And so the King spares my life for one more day, so that he might hear the rest of my dark tale.

As soon as I finish a story... I begin a new one... like the one that you, dear reader, have before you now.

Prologue

Dear Legion,

First, thanks tons for going into hiding outside the mortal world. I got to hunt you down big, bad wolf style—my favorite kind of hunting. Even better, you shacked up in an ancient realm without Wi-Fi. Now I get to communicate with you via robo-pigeons. Yay for me. BTW, the birds are "priceless," and weren't built to help me "score" with my "adult-boyhood crush" blah, blah, blah, so please don't destroy the mechanical flock in a fit of pique.

Decorating hack: repurpose the robo-pigeons as knickknacks to create a steampunk vibe. Not so I can watch you through the eye-cams. (Wink.)

Second, it's sometimes impossible to judge someone's tone in a letter. Since I'm anti-misunderstandings, I'd like to clear things up right from the start. TONE: dry as a desert mixed with a dash of frothing-at-the-mouth rage.

Clear as crystal? Or mud?

Third, I refuse to call you "Honey," the name your friends are using. Babycakes, I'm not your friend, I'm your potential obsession. And, to be brutally honest about the matter, I'd rather call you Sugar Tits McGyna while having my wings ripped from my back (again) than refer to you as "Honey." A name you like only because you hate the girl you used to be. News flash: I like the old Legion. (Leggie. Legs. ←I'm trying out new nicknames for you. Did we just find a winner?) The old you gifted me with your virginity in a bar bathroom five minutes after meeting me. Or was it four? I always forget. What's not to like about *that*?

Sure, you only slept with me so you could savagely murder me after

I got you off, thereby protecting Aeron, the man you truly desired. And yeah, okay, I probably deserve a couple dozen more murder attempts because I later abducted your pregnant friend in an unethical-ish power play. But every couple has their issues, right?

I'm willing to attend a counseling sesh with you. Can you say the same? Please?

FYI, my crew is on stand-by, ready to ~~kidnap~~ ~~abduct~~ borrow a world-renowned shrink at a moment's notice. All I need from you is a *yes*.

Lastly, I know you've been to hell and back—literally. I know you were hurt and abused in the worst ways. TONE: soft as a damn feather. I'm sorry for everything you've endured. If you really want to hurt the ones who hurt you, embrace happiness. Don't let the past ruin your future.

Please, give me a chance to get to know the new you. A chance to help you heal, if I can. I think about you constantly, dream about you every night, and crave you every second of every day.

Yours forever,

Galen the Magnificent

PS: In pages 2-35 of this letter you'll find pictures of severed demon heads. Because of the mystical shield around your cabin, I can't lay your dead enemies/tormenters at your feet. Instead, I have to settle for laying photos of their decapitated heads upon your desk. (Sorry, but gift exchanges are against Galen-policy.)

PPS: I'm a wanted man in more ways than one. Fine. Two. Two ways. 1) someone put a measly ten million dollar contract on my life. (I promise I'm worth more. Ask every woman I've ever dated, then ask every woman hoping to date me in the future.) 2) if you read between the lines, you'll realize I'm hinting in a super subtle way that a megaton of other women find me irresistible, and I won't always be on the meat market. Snap up this grade A filet while you've got the chance.

* * * *

Yo! Leigh. LeeLee. (← Yes? No? Maybe I should just stick with the classic—Legion.)

A week has passed since you received letter #1, and in return I've gotten zilch, zero, nada. I can only assume you're still reeling over the poetry-like beauty of my words. And that's not the demon of False

Hope talking. Sure, the fiend bunks inside my head with his good pal, Jealousy, and the two bastards love to build me up and tear me down, but come on! You can't deny I've got the wings of an angel, and the face and body of a Greek god. And not an old, decrepit one, either, but a real smoke show.

Admit it. If we were characters in a (super hot) romance novel, you'd be the vulnerable babe in need of a protector, and I'd be the hardcore alpha villain everyone secretly yearns to tame. Spoiler alert: I'm willing to let you give the taming thing your best shot. Because I'm a giver.

TONE: 100% dead-as-roadkill serious.

I know you don't want to see me because I'm "dangerous," "deranged," and "possibly the worst being ever created by Zeus—or anyone." But underneath this chiseled, bronzed exterior beats a heart of gold, probably. You'll never know the truth unless you come out of hiding and take another peek under my hood.

Come on...take another peek... This time, try not to scratch my priceless exterior. Kidding, only kidding. I want you to scratch my exterior—mostly my *post*erior—I just don't want you to rip out my engine with your bare claws.

I promise I will never hurt you. I will only hurt other people...a lot of other people...like, countless other people, but NEVER you. So, what do you say? Will you go on the best date of your life with me?

Yours,

Galen the Eager

PS: I know I'm giving you the hard sell here, but I'm certain you'll thank me later.

* * * *

My dearest Honey,

What can I do to prove myself to you? Or at least get a response? I'd be happy with a single word on the dusty window. Wait. Shit! You weren't taught to read or write when you lived in hell, were you?

Well. That sucks donkey balls. How am I supposed to let you know there's no line I won't cross for you, no deed too dark?

At least you don't have to hear today's tone: humiliatingly earnest.

Whatever. I'm still going to finish this letter just in case I'm wrong.

The war raging between Hades and Lucifer is spreading through different realms in the underworld and even spilling into the mortal world. Every day the battles grow more violent. I know you consider Hades a friend, and think he's protecting you and all—and he is, for the moment—but sooner or later, the violence WILL reach your door, and you'll be on your own.

I don't want you on your own.

If you leave with me, you'll get 24/7 care, and a huge benefits package. I can't oversell that benefits package. Your safety, well-being, and satisfaction in a job well done will be my top priorities, I swear it.

I want to protect you. I NEED to protect you. Please, let me.

If you're afraid of me…please, don't be afraid of me. I'm a changed man. Well, maybe not changed, per se. "Changed" suggests there was something wrong with the old, perfect me. But. I'm considering the possibility of maybe thinking about becoming a *tweaked* man. You know, being even more perfect.

I'm not asking for a chance this time. I'm begging for one.

Yours,

Galen the Desperate

PS: If you think I'm hot, charming, and a treasure worth fighting for, do NOT reply to this message.

Chapter One

Possessed by the two worst demons imaginable. Villain extraordinaire. Lover of cheap wines and expensive women. Angel impersonator. Immortal assassin. Absentee dad to a twenty-something Harpy who hated his guts for a thousand different reasons. Galen was all of those things, and more.

Most people had a demon on one shoulder and a cherub on the other. He had two demons—False Hope and Jealousy. In other words, he had a corruptionscience rather than a conscience. The fiends fed on destruction, and they were always ravenous.

Throughout the endless eons of his existence, he'd lied to friends and enemies alike, cheated without a second thought, stolen whatever he desired, and killed with wild abandon. *Play by the rules, and lose to a rule breaker.*

He broke the rules better than anyone.

He would do *anything* to protect what he valued. Maybe because there were so few things he actually valued? At the top of the short list was his friend and adopted daughter Fox, who was—ironically enough—the keeper of Distrust yet the only person he trusted. In second place, his many homes. In the final slot, Legion. If she'd given him any encouragement, she would have moved to #2. But nooooo. Persistently stubborn, she continued to deny their connection. Plus, she distracted the shit out of him.

In a way, she reminded him of his demons. Which made sense. Once upon a time, Legion had been a daughter of hell—a literal demon—working 9 to 5 torturing souls. A true cutthroat business. To become human and retain her immortality, she'd made a deal with Lucifer, the Prince of Darkness.

Galen suspected the deal had somehow included the loss of *his* sanity.

From the beginning, his obsession with Legion had proved baffling. Always before, he'd gravitated to bad girls who pretended to be good. Maybe because *he'd* pretended to be a good guy for centuries—a literal angel—and he'd seen himself in his lovers.

So, basically, he'd dated himself?

Yeah, the logic checked out 100%. What wasn't to love about a supervillain willing to do anything to accomplish a task or crush a goal?

Legion was the exact opposite: a good girl pretending to be bad. But even still, this particular pretender had two superpowers no one else had ever possessed. 1) the ability to make Galen focus on the future, his shitshow of past and present inconsequential. 2) the ability to strip away layers of hard won sophistication, leaving a primitive caveman desperate for sex.

How did she do it?

Like you don't know. If ever Galen had created a woman from scratch, he would have used Legion as the template. She had the dangerous curves of a femme fatale, topped off with a silky waterfall of dark blonde curls his hands itched to fist. Black spiky lashes framed eyes the color of whiskey—eyes just as intoxicating. Lush red lips tempted all who gazed upon them, silently promising to escort sinners to heaven.

Her personality only added to her appeal. With a tantalizing vicious streak, an affinity for anything princess, surprising strengths, and agonizing vulnerabilities, she suited needs Galen had never known he'd had.

He *needed* to get her into his bed. Gentleman extraordinaire, he would only keep her there a few months. Maybe a few years. A mere blip when you were immortal. After he'd touched and tasted every inch of her, taken her in every position imaginable, and brought her to climax, oh, about a thousand times, her effect on him would be neutralized, probably, and he could focus his energy on war. So simple. So easy.

But first, he had to save her life.

Earlier tonight, one of Galen's enemies had sent an army to abduct Fox. An attempt to hobble him, since she was more than a friend; she was his right-hand woman. The list of potential suspects contained only two names.

--Lucifer, prick to the max

--Cronus, former Titan king who'd died…kind of

The attempt hadn't ended as the bastard had hoped. Whichever bastard happened to be responsible. Fox had gotten away with only minor wear and tear. Galen remained irked. Because, as an encore, his enemy decided to abduct Legion, a fragile flower who withered at the first hint of violence. Not counting the time she'd tried to murder Galen, of course.

A god or king going to all this effort, simply to strike at big, bad Galen? Or maybe the culprit wanted to force his hand. A *do this or the girl dies* kind of thing.

Hey, asshole. Galen from Ancient Greece called. He wants his plan back.

Galen would find and behead the POS. *After* he slaughtered the horde of immortal soldiers marching toward Legion's cabin. Priorities.

Your efforts are in vain. You can't save her. The soldiers will find her first. She'll die cursing your name…

He ground his teeth. *Hate False Hope!* The fiend perverted true hope, inciting fear—a twisted hope for the worst to happen. *I will do anything, cross any line, to reach Legion before the soldiers.*

Determined, he rushed around gnarled trees, pushed past tangled limbs, and jumped over massive buttress roots. Sweat trickled from his temples, beaded on the back of his neck, and ran in rivulets down the muscles in his torso. The scent of pine and jasmine clung to his skin while leaves and insects burrowed in his wings.

Wings, man. The snow white, feathery monstrosities were both a blessing and a curse. His appearance said, *Come closer, touch…* The moment someone complied—boom! Galen would strike. Very few people knew he'd only grown the wings after his demon-possession. A gift from False Hope.

Re-gift, anyone?

Though Galen had exceptional night vision honed from centuries of training, he could not see through the thick, pervasive darkness that currently cloaked the realm. If not for the crimson laser shooting from the eyes of his robo guide pigeon, he would have been blinded. Soon, the sun would rise and the soldiers would have the advantage.

Faster! He'd been sprinting for hours. Now, extreme exhaustion plagued him. His lungs burned as if he inhaled acid rather than oxygen, and his limbs trembled so fervently, his bones felt like tuning forks. Blisters had formed and burst on his feet, filling his combat boots with blood. His heart hammered against his ribs at warp-speed, setting the pace for his legs. *Almost there.*

The closer he got to Legion, the better he scented her. Wildflowers and temptation.

He could reach her quicker if he could fly, but air-piranha greeted anyone who dared soar above the treetops. Beasts able to eat a man's flesh and muscle in seconds, leaving only bones and death. Galen knew because he'd once tossed a man up there. *My bad.*

Flashing—moving from one place to another with only a thought—wasn't an option, either. The moment you materialized in another location, the air-piranha materialized around you.

Galen had visited this forested labyrinth countless times, attempting every conceivable means of reaching Legion. In the end, he'd only managed to memorize a route to the cabin while on foot, no matter where he happened to be.

He had yet to bypass the biggest obstacle. The mystical wards that surrounded the cabin.

Anyone who stepped on the cabin's porch prayed for death. Galen knew this firsthand.

Which was why he'd resorted to sending handwritten messages via robo-birds instead of, say, sending a strip-o-gram starring his majestic majesticness.

Maybe the army-o-enemies would have better luck with the wards, the sheer number of bodies overwhelming the magic, maybe not. Any chance over .000% was too great. For Legion's sake, Galen had to be the first, the only, to succeed.

A steady *thump-thump* of footsteps sounded, breaking into his thoughts. Well, well. He'd caught up with the army at last. Time for stage two of Operation Kill Everyone.

Galen palmed two short-swords and quickened his pace.

"What is *that?*" The speaker had picked up Galen's panting breaths and heavy footfalls.

"Hold," someone else called. The thumping ceased. "Prepare for attack."

Clothing rustled, bodies shifting. Metal whistled, weapons being readied.

Too infuriated for finesse, Galen burst past a line of trees. With the robo-pigeon's help, he catalogued his opponents. Forty-three men wearing bloodstained armor. Forty of the SOBs held swords, three clutched torches. The soldiers had broken into groups of four and stood shoulder to shoulder, each member facing a different direction.

Let's do this.

Almost frothing at the mouth, Galen dive-bombed one group, knocking the four males into a second group. As they tangled together, he flared his wings. The enormous appendages would have made him a bigger target, if he hadn't spun. The razors he'd woven into the tips of the feathers sliced one throat after another. A battle hack he'd learned from a warrior named Puck the Undefeated.

For the next few minutes, Galen played a game he liked to call War Santa. *A severed spine for you. Disembowelment for you. A boot to the testicles for you.* He kicked again, ensuring said testicles got a one-way ticket into the guy's chest cavity.

The gift recipients grunted, groaned, and bellowed. With a little follow-up slice and dice, they also died. A rusted copper tang saturated the too-hot breeze, colliding with other *eau de* battle scents: emptied bowels, urine, and acrid sweat.

When the last soldier fell, Galen went after the torch-holders. The torches fell, too, a golden blaze quickly spreading over grass, trees, and bodies like, well, wildfire. Agonized screams echoed through the night, survivors doing their best to douse the flames.

As Galen oversaw his next kill, pain erupted in his shoulder. He glanced down. An arrow had embedded in the space between his collarbone and heart. *Poisoned?* Dizziness rushed through his head and stars winked through his vision.

He almost missed the sword aimed at his throat. Block. Turn. Swing.

Can't fail. Keep fighting.

Injured soldiers climbed to their feet to attack. Round two. Galen ducked and spun, simultaneously hitting the end of the arrow with his own sword hilt to send the shaft out the other side. Then he came up swinging. *Clang. Whoosh. Clink.*

Despite the pain and dizziness, his ferocity and cruelty never wavered.

Jealousy said, *These men covet what's mine. They must die.*

For once, Galen and the demon agreed.

Chapter Two

"Time to make a decision, once and for all." Legion paced from one side of the living room to the other, the walls of the cabin seeming to shrink around her. Deep breath in, out. "Having the right name is important." Especially when you'd once been an object passed around for the use of others. "But having *two* names is confusing. Am I Legion or Honey? I think of myself as Legion, but *legion* means a multitude, as if I'm just one in a crowd of thousands. But *honey* is a healthy substitute for sugar, and I'm a substitute for no one. I much prefer high fructose corn syrup, the Cadillac of sweeteners." Gah! "At this point, maybe Hey You would work."

Her roommate Tipsy—aka Sips—chittered in response. He was a pain in the butt runt of a raccoon that Hades rescued from a bar parking lot.

The evolution of the little cutie's nickname never failed to amuse. *Tipsy... Tippy Poo...Tippy...Tip Tip... Tip Tip Hooray... Tippy Tippy Boom Boom...Tippy Sippy...Lord Sippy...Sips.* Except today. Nothing amused her today.

"Maybe I should wave the white towel of surrender." She frowned. The phrasing struck her as odd. But then, mortal references had always confused her. "Maybe I should go with a certain male's suggestion, and forever refer to myself as Sugar Tits McGyna. Although I can imagine the response I'll get from others. *Hey MyVagina. Come over here and pour your Sugar on me.*" No, thanks.

Why did a name even matter anymore, anyway? She never interacted with anyone other than Sips.

But she *wanted* to interact with someone else...

He Who Should Not Be Named.

Legion would have exited the cabin and hunted him down, maybe, but probably not, if foreboding hadn't prickled the back of her neck, telling her to stay in, go nowhere, and speak to no one. Outside these walls, pain and only pain awaited her. No doubt about it.

Did she really want to kick off a new season of night terrors? She'd finally started sleeping again.

All right. It was settled, then. She would stay in and torment herself about a moniker, and refuse—absolutely refuse!—to ponder the beautiful man who had inspired the debate about it.

Beautiful?

Ha! Try sadistic. Sinister. Maddening. There was nothing beautiful about those things. Although, yes, okay, she'd once *loved* those qualities in a person. Fine! A part of her still did. But only when the person used those qualities against her enemies.

Anyway. A new name wouldn't change who or what she was. *Quinientos Dieciséis of the Croisé Sombres of Neid and Notpe-hocil.* The title given to her at birth.

The mix of languages, words, and numbers literally translated to "Legion Five Hundred and Sixteen of the Dark Crusaders of Envy and Need." One of a myriad demons assigned to punish humans who'd committed crimes motivated by jealousy.

She gasped as the hem of her ball gown snagged on a splintered piece of wood and tore. Stupid gown! Why did she have to love and adore impractical prom-wear so much? Why did she even want to feel pretty? She had no one to impress. She'd loved, and she'd lost.

Don't think about that, either. Unless you want to start sobbing?

Desperate for a distraction, she focused on the cabin. Home sweet home. She'd been here for…a while. She'd lost track of time. Though small, the place was a total dream. Weathered white wood. Crystal chandeliers. Stained glass. Every piece of furniture had a rustic yet chic flare.

She had only to tell the refrigerator what she desired and voilà, the food magically appeared. Same with the wardrobe in her bedroom. Legion wanted for nothing…except for peace of mind. And self-esteem. And, you know, a life worth living.

Okay, so the distraction hadn't worked. Wagging a finger at Sips, she said, "Stop planning ways to torture me, and start helping me."

The raccoon perched on a floral-print couch, watching her. Every day he played some kind of prank. Pebbles in her shoes. Snakes or scorpions in her bed. Urinating on her clothes. But dang if he wasn't the most adorable creature ever.

"Forget my name. I have another decision to make. To date or not to date..." *Do it. Say it.* "Galen." There. He Who Should Not Be Named had been named.

Had she inadvertently summoned him the way humans had once summoned her?

Heart thudding, she spun and searched the cabin for any sign of him. Nope. No sign. She breathed a sigh of relief. Yep. Relief. Not disappointment.

"In the plus column, he's an immortal warrior. Outrageously strong. He can kill anyone who threatens me. In the minus column, he's known as the Betrayer. How can I ever trust him?"

Chitter-chitter. Sips-speak for *All pluses. Why does such a fine specimen want YOU?*

"Excellent question." Pacing, pacing. At their first meeting, she'd tried to kill Galen. Why would he give her a second chance to strike? Unless he planned to strike at *her*?

No, no. He'd had plenty of opportunities to do so. Instead, he'd only ever protected her. He'd even faced the wrath of her first love, Aeron, just to spend time with her. Galen genuinely wanted her. And, well, she'd grown *flattered* by his attention.

"Okay, I'm going to give you the full scoop, nothing held back." Maybe she would stumble upon answers to her dilemmas. Trying to ignore the issues hadn't helped. *Here goes.* "Forever ago, I fell in love with Aeron Lord, an immortal warrior once possessed by the demon of Wrath. I was fully demon back then, and I knew I couldn't win him. So I made a bargain with Lucifer to acquire a human body *and* keep my immortality *and* retain my demonic defenses. Like my poisonous bite and claws. The best of both worlds. In exchange, I had a limited time to seduce Aeron into my bed. Failure meant returning to hell... as Lucifer's slave. I might have won, if Aeron hadn't been busy falling for Olivia, the Sent One supposed to kill him."

Chitter-chitter. *Now there is a good, solid name with lots of nickname potential. Liv. Oli. Olive. Via.*

"Are you even listening to me?" Legion demanded with a stomp of her foot.

You resent Aeron for rejecting you, yada yada.

Well, he wasn't wrong. "With time running out, I made one more attempt to win Aeron's heart… by *stopping* the heart of his greatest enemy, Galen. I know, I know. A heart is a super cliché gift. But come on! It was my first romantic gesture."

Finally! Things are getting interesting. Go on.

"I tracked Galen to a mortal bar, and lured him into the ladies' bathroom, where I kissed him. To distract him. But that man knows what to do with his tongue. Once we started sucking face, I only wanted more. So, me being me, I took more. I took everything. He popped my berry. That's what humans call the losing of one's virginity, yes?"

Sips snickered. *You nailed it. Galen popped your berry good.*

'Good' did not begin to describe it. "Afterward, I got my act together and bit him, injecting him with my venom. But deep down I think I kinda sorta wanted him to survive. Not that it mattered either way. Aeron picked Olivia, and I lost the bet with Lucifer."

Legion staved off a well of tears. The Prince of Darkness had beaten and violated her in the worst ways. Then he'd let his armies do the same.

Memories surged, unbidden. *Hands tied behind my back. A gag stuffed into my mouth. Clothing ripped away. Laughter abounding.*

Her throat constricted, cutting off her airway. The things the demons had done to her…the way they'd taunted her…all the sickening ways they'd broken her spirit, soul, and body.

Aeron and a few others had come to her rescue, but by then, she'd been a shell of herself.

Poor Legion. A porcelain doll, shattered into a million little pieces.

Her gaze found the letters Galen had mailed via the robotic birds, the pages stacked on a bright pink desk. She'd drafted and trashed countless replies. What could she tell him, really? The day she'd met him was the last time she'd experienced excitement. She'd had fun with him.

She'd forgotten for a while, but now that she'd remembered… she craved more. *Needed* more. There was a slight problem, hardly worth mentioning, but, uh, the thought of being with a man, any man, made her physically ill.

"Galen is a bad person," she said. "The worst of the worst. He needs someone who has a moral compass. My compass is kind of broken. Or nonexistent." Raised in hell, she'd learned that harming others was a privilege, and screams of agony the perfect lullaby. If you kept your word, you were a fool in need of punishment. If you intentionally helped someone, you were a fool in need of punishment. If you told the truth, you were—yep—a fool in need of punishment. "He's conceited, arrogant, and a total douche…but still I want to give him a chance. Why?"

Chitter. Possible translation: *You hate the person you've become. Deep down, you know the only way to have a different life is to do something different. Galen certainly qualifies as different.*

Or maybe the proper translation was: *You dumb.*

"To go on a single date with Galen, I'll have to leave the cabin for good." Here, she felt brave, like the Legion of old. Outside, she feared *everything.* "The second I leave, I'll negate Hades's wards." He'd said he'd owed someone a favor and that, by aiding Legion, he'd fulfilled his obligation, and therefore would never waste time reactivating the wards. "Is being with Galen worth abandoning the protection of the cabin?"

Only if you enjoy pleasure.

She did. And she didn't. Physically ill, remember?

Sighing, she adjusted the tiara pinned to her braids. Sparkle—a mandatory addition to every girl's wardrobe. "It *would* be nice to have a supportive partner." The way Aeron worshiped and adored Olivia…

On paper, the couple seemed odd. The innocent angel and the erotic demon. In person, they fit together seamlessly.

"Aeron has become a brother to me. A lollipop of man-candy, sure, but still a brother. It's just…he used to make me feel safe." Now? The honor belonged to the cabin. A one-sided pairing. But Galen had potential. He was so incredibly strong, he could hold her with one muscular arm and keep the world at bay with the other. "The difference is, I can trust what I feel with Aeron, but I can't trust *anything* I feel with Galen."

What was real, and what was manufactured by his demons?

A strange stillness came over Sips, the hairs on his back standing at attention. Tension thickened the air.

"What's wrong?" she rasped, her heart jumping.

His claws tapped against the wooden floor as he crossed the living room. He leaped and landed on the windowsill, then peered out the glass. The sun had begun to rise, casting muted golden beams over the forest outside.

Chitter, chitter. *Uh-oh. Incoming.*

The front door burst open, wood shards raining down. Legion gasped. A bloody Galen loomed in the opening, a scowl twisting his face.

Her knees knocked together, a mix of fear and fascination storming through her. Galen. Here.

As tall and pumped-up with muscle as always, but not as immaculate. Tangled white-blond hair and ocean-water eyes glittered with menace and pain. Blood splattered his shirt and leather pants.

She'd called him beautiful, but she'd been wrong. He. Was. Exquisite. The muted sunlight created a halo-effect, turning him into a fallen angel. Sinister, treacherous—and clearly in pain. The moment he'd stepped onto the porch, he'd had to go toe-to-toe with Hades's wards.

According to her landlord, those wards would make a man feel as if his head was a bread bowl filled with brain soup.

She gulped. "Wh-what are you doing here?"

"Rescuing you," Galen grated, his voice deep, husky, and anguished. "Let's go."

Wires in her brain seemed to flicker to life, reminding her of something she'd once learned about this man. Long ago, he'd strapped his immortals to a table for weeks or months at a time, cut out different organs, and placed those organs in jars so the victim could always see them.

Go with *that* guy? "No," she said. *Do not panic. Remain calm, aware, and alert.* Her dagger. Where was her dagger?

"If you want to live," he said, stepping inside the cabin, "you'll come with me. Now."

Chapter Three

Galen hadn't seen Legion in so long, the sight of her affected him on a deep, primitive level. Like a punch to the soul. With spiked metal gloves.

Her beauty stole his breath.

Shock and lust momentarily overshadowed the throbbing pain in his temples. Those damn wards. As he fought their mystical hold, he drank in all that was Legion Honey. A waterfall of dark blonde hair, topped by a diamond tiara. Those whiskey-brown eyes now wide with astonishment. Those perfect heart-shaped lips remained parted, as if desperate for a kiss.

She had the face of an angel and the body of a porn star, and he wanted to pray and sin at the same time.

Despite the gravity of their situation, Galen took the time to give her luscious body the languid once-over it deserved. As she panted, her plump breasts rose and fell with rapid succession. Her nipples beaded. She wore an elaborate pink ball gown with a corset top and plunging neckline, the skirt embroidered with roses. On her feet—furry house-boots. A sapphire choker circled her neck, and multiple ruby bands adorned her wrists, adding another layer of sweetness to the whole saint-and-sinner package.

No question, this woman had been created with Galen's seduction—and downfall—in mind.

His knees quaked, threatening to buckle. As his level of pain intensified, his eyesight hazed. He swallowed a roar of fury and frustration. *Not done looking at Legion!*

Determined to reach his quarry, to save her, he fought more fervently. *Stay upright. Ignore the aches. Push one foot forward, then the other...*

Finally! Movement. Muscles unlocked from bone, and he stumbled into the foyer.

The wards fought back, hard, melting his brain. Something warm and wet dripped from his eyes…his nose…his ears. He frowned and reached up, his fingers trembling. A swift swipe revealed copious amounts of blood.

Both demons wailed, the pain cutting through *them*.

Legion looked Galen over and flinched. Voice hoarse, she said, "I wasn't sure…I thought I could…I can't! You should leave. You *must* leave."

"Not going…anywhere…without you." The pain crested, searing agony consuming every inch of him. Still he moved forward, stumbling deeper into the cabin. A surge of adrenaline acted as fuel, keeping him on his feet. "There's another army…coming for you."

The color drained from her face as she scrambled away from him. A reaction he abhorred with every fiber of his being. He longed to shout, *Do not run from me. Come closer.*

"*Another* army?" she said between wheezing breaths.

"I slaughtered the first. You're welcome."

A raccoon jumped off the window, inspected Galen up and down, and yawned. There was something odd about the animal, though. An energy he'd never before encountered.

No time to ponder the reason. A brutal force knocked him to his knees, a brand new pain lancing the arch of his wing. He'd been plugged by an arrow, he realized.

Well, hell. The second army had arrived.

He glanced over his shoulder. Roughly a mile away, soldiers exited the forest and unleashed a volley of spears. With a curse, Galen slammed the door shut.

Thunk, thunk, thunk.

The tips came out the other side. He moved to the center of the room while yanking the projectile out of his wing. A river of crimson gushed from the wound.

"We are minutes from invasion," he grated.

"Impossible. This is a trick." She rushed around him to peer out the window. Shudders wracked her. "The soldiers probably work for you."

Galen followed and glanced over her shoulder. Sunlight illuminated more than a hundred men with crossbows, swords, and spears.

"You think I'd ever allow my men to harm me?" he snapped.

The next shudder nearly knocked her off her feet. "All right. Yes. Just...stay here. I'll grab my go-bag."

"Leave everything behind."

Fury exploded in her eyes. "My jewels. Mine."

A show of spirit, over jewelry? Color him intrigued. He held up his hands, palms out. "Do what you must. But hurry."

Realizing she'd all but challenged him, she withered. Then she sprinted from the room, the soft pitter-patter of her footsteps resonating.

What if she ditched him?

No matter. *I will find her.*

Palming two daggers, he scanned the living room. A homey nook with well-loved furniture: a floral print couch, two recliners, a coffee table with golden turtles under each leg, and a fluffy ottoman. Posters decorated the walls, each one depicting a different forest animal in lingerie.

Some kind of raccoon porn?

On both sides of the marble hearth, bookcases displayed a collection of how-to guides and fiction. How to read, how to utilize proper etiquette, how to "grammar properly," and the complete collection of works by Jill Monroe, Kresley Cole, and PC Cast.

In the far corner was a cluttered desk. Beside it, a small trashcan with one... five... ten...fifteen crumpled up pieces of paper. Curiosity got the better of him. The ends of his wings brushed the floor as he stalked over, every step a new lesson in anguish.

Ignore the pain. Focus on the papers, the words.

When he read the first two words—*Dear Galen*—shock jolted him. Legion *could* read and write, and she *had* responded to him, she just hadn't mailed them via robo-express. Knowing she hadn't left him hanging soothed his heart. In a totally manly way. Super manly.

He'd never been a good guy, but what the hell. He would do Legion a major solid and hand-deliver the letters to himself, saving her time and postage. He stuffed as many sheets of paper as possible underneath his shirt. Because why not? Perfect timing. Legion returned, a backpack slung over her shoulder.

He confiscated the pack. Or tried to. She growled at him and snapped, "Mine!"

She *really* liked her jewels. Got it.

When she spotted his blood-soaked daggers, she lost her fire. She opened her mouth, then closed it, only a strangled sound escaping.

He fought a scowl. "These blades will never harm you. They will only ever protect you."

The tension didn't leave her. She scooped up the raccoon before croaking, "We're ready."

Even more baggage. Perfect. "We'll go out the back door and—"

"No." Once again, she went from kitten to lioness in .02 seconds. "You will follow me."

He almost smiled. How he'd missed her passion and zest for life.

She hurried through the small cabin and stopped inside a bedroom, where she kicked a rug out of the way, revealing a hidden latch. "There's a tunnel below the house."

"Where does it lead?"

"A mortal dimension with creepy-ass rodents. Hades's words, not mine. He says this is an emergency escape hatch only." She chewed on her bottom lip, glancing from the hatch to the door. "Maybe we should split up. You know, to better our odds of success. I'll take the tunnel, and you take the back door. Okay? Yes?"

He narrowed his eyes. "Do you want to survive the coming attack?"

She gulped as if he'd just issued a threat. Nodded.

"Then we stay together." Injured muscles protested as he opened the latch. Rusted hinges popped and warped wood groaned, a murky pit soon revealed.

Dust motes danced up, up, carrying a musty odor. Light spilled from a lantern that hung from a wall hook, highlighting a set of decrepit stairs. The bottom...too dark to see.

"Climb down and wait for me," he commanded. He would have preferred to go first and clear the way, if necessary, but Legion wasn't strong enough to close the hatch.

"Climb down...by myself? You were right. We need to stick together." Sweat beaded on her brow and upper lip, while her cheeks bleached of color. "I—I...can't be trapped...won't..."

He understood her panicked reaction. Trauma could forever alter your reaction to old and new situations. "I once spent a hundred years trapped in a grave," he said. "Feeling helpless isn't my idea of a good time, either, but there's no time to argue."

Footsteps resounded in the distance, the army closing in fast.

Galen ripped the sheet from the bed, tied one end around the hatch's handle and fisted the other end, then yanked Legion against the hard line of his body, careful not to smash the freeloading raccoon. She gasped—unsurprising. The shocker? She also melted against him, as if suddenly comforted by his presence. The feel of her...

Focus! Right. He tightened his hold—and jumped into the pit.

As they fell, the sheet pulled taut and the lid closed with a heavy thud, sealing them inside the tomb-like tunnel. The light in the lantern snuffed out.

When the sheet lost all slack, the material ripped from his grip. He flared his injured wings, despite the pain, attempting to slow their momentum, but the walls were too close together, and he accomplished nothing. Left with no other recourse, he enfolded Legion inside the soft cushion provided by his feathers and angled their bodies, ensuring he would be the one to—

Impact!

He hit first. Legion smashed into him, the heavy backpack adding to her weight. Numerous bones snapped. His wings broke and twisted. Multiple organs ruptured, a new round of agony searing him. The taste of old pennies coated his tongue, and he was pretty sure blood leaked from his every orifice.

"You okay?" The words were slurred, and he realized he'd bitten off half his tongue.

"I'm okay, I'm okay," she rushed out. "Sips?"

The raccoon said, "Eeeee, eeeee."

He'd take that to mean, *I'm fine.*

Galen spit out a mouthful of blood, the piece of tongue, and maybe a tooth. Releasing Legion, he labored to unsteady legs. Dizziness flooded him, and stars winked across his sightline. *Must remain conscious. Can't pass out until my woman is safe.*

My woman? As if we are a done deal?

As his eyes adjusted to the gloom, he noticed flickering light about a hundred feet ahead. He took Legion's hand and kicked into motion, taking stock of his surroundings along the way. The tunnel reminded him of an old, abandoned subway station. Graffiti on the walls, rats scurrying this way and that. Nothing creepy-ass about—

Nope. Never mind. The rats had horns. And fangs. And forked tails.

With his free hand, he dug the cell phone out of his pocket and fired off a text to Fox.

Probs dying, def being chased. Need pick up for 2 ASAP

He'd trained himself to text blindfolded, and with one hand, whether left or right. He also paid handsomely to use mystical Wi-Fi, so he could message anyone, any time. Note to self: add Legion to his monthly bill.

The phone vibrated. He glanced at the screen, and relief washed over him.

Fox: **Did my baby boy get an owie? No worries, I'll track & find you**

Cheeky little wench. But then, they'd been together for centuries, had seen the best in each other, and the worst. Had fought side-by-side, and saved each other countless times.

Fox was a Gatekeeper, able to open a portal anywhere. A secret they'd kept for centuries. Gatekeepers had a limited lifespan known as a rotation. Roughly two thousand years. When she'd reached the end of her rotation, Galen had helped her acquire the demon of Distrust to ensure she lived forever.

It hadn't taken long for the demon to begin changing her personality, as Galen had expected. Fewer smiles and jokes. Darker temper tantrums. *Much* darker. Moments of black-out rage.

A small price to pay to stay together.

They'd met in Ancient Greece, a time when Galen had warred with the Lords of the Underworld. Thirteen immortal warriors possessed by demons of their own. Aeron, Torin, Maddox, Amun, Reyes, Baden, Strider, Paris, Cameo, Gideon, Kane, Lucien, and Sabin. Once his closest friends and allies. Then his greatest enemies. Now…friends again?

As Galen ushered Legion through the tunnel, his life flashed before his eyes, different memories playing through his mind.

--The time of his "birth." Zeus, supreme sovereign of Greek gods, created a host of warriors to act as his personal guard. Men and women willing to destroy anyone who threatened their leader.

--Zeus deciding to entrust one guard—Pandora—with a mysterious box made of bone, causing jealousy to spread through the ranks like wildfire.

Galen had questioned the king about the decision. He'd never forgotten the response. *Should I place my most treasured possession in your hands? You, the most disappointing of my children. Do you think your hesitation to render a deathblow has gone unnoticed?*

Back then, he'd wondered why they killed rather than incarcerated.

Why waste a life? Wasn't redemption possible?

Now he knew better. Be the one to slay, or get slain. There was no middle ground.

--Galen deciding to prove his worth by stealing and opening the box, and inviting his friends to participate.

--Entertaining second thoughts, wondering how could they betray Pandora so blatantly.

--Asking the other warriors to stand down. They'd refused.

--In a snit, and confessing the plan to Zeus.

But the warning had come too late. Maddox had already opened the box, unleashing a horde of demons upon an unsuspecting world.

As punishment, Zeus forced each Lord to host a single demon. Except for Galen, of course, since he'd instigated the entire mess.

--Being kicked from the heavens, the other Lords banding together to shun Galen.

--The demons devouring Galen's good sense.

He'd created an army of humans hell-bent on annihilating "evil" immortals.

--Finding and caring for Fox, a five-year-old orphan with an ability he'd hoped to one day exploit, then falling in love with her somewhere along the way.

--Finding out he had a daughter by blood. Gwendolyn, a beautiful Harpy who'd married Sabin, demon keeper of Doubt.

Guilt pricked the back of his neck. He'd treated Gwen like garbage, knowing a connection to him often equated to a death sentence.

--Meeting Legion and calling a cease fire with the Lords, ending their centuries' old feud. He even had an open-ish invitation to crash at their place whenever needed.

Wait. Why was he reliving these things? *Am I dying?*

The tremors in his limbs intensified, and he stumbled. If not for Legion, he would have toppled. Though she looked delicate, she had enough strength to keep him upright.

"Maybe we should rest?" she said, panting.

He spit out another mouthful of blood before grunting a denial.

She readjusted the backpack's strap, the weight of it only adding to their burden. Again he tried to claim it. Again she refused. Very well.

The faint squeak of rotted wood echoed as different soldiers descended the steps. Great! The army had followed them into the tunnel.

Up ahead, a spear of azure light sliced through the air. The fabric of time and space peeled back to reveal a doorway into another realm. Fox stood on the other side, tall and slender with jet-black hair and arresting features. She wore a halter top and black leather pants, and clutched a dagger in each hand; she looked every inch the bad ass. No woman fought dirtier, or impressed Galen more.

Relief provided a final surge of strength. He pumped his legs faster…faster.

Fox spotted Legion and cursed. The two had met once before, after Galen had kidnapped Legion's friend Ashlyn—wife to Maddox, keeper of Violence. Legion had offered herself in trade. At the time, she'd feared Galen and hated Fox. The feeling had been mutual for Fox, who abhorred weakness of any kind.

Galen usually abhorred weakness, too. But. When it came to Legion, nothing mattered but the woman herself.

"Hurry." Fox waved him on while peering over his shoulder. "They're gaining on you."

A tremor pitched Legion against him. She attempted a backward glance, but Galen pushed past the spike of pain—*too much, too much, breathe*—and flared his broken wings, blocking her view. No reason to frighten her further. At the same time, he gathered her closer and pressed her face into the hollow of his neck.

Sips protested the close proximity, scratching the hell out of Galen's pec.

"Behave, young man," Legion muttered. "I mean, young boy. I mean, young raccoon. Galen is trying to save us."

Trying? No. Succeeding? Yes.

At last, they slipped through the mystical doorway, entering one of his many private realms. His favorite. A fortress built to withstand any natural or supernatural disaster.

The moment the portal closed, blocking out the soldiers, Legion's safety guaranteed, Galen collapsed, welcoming the cloud of darkness that swallowed him whole.

Chapter Four

Legion watched, wide-eyed, as Fox dragged Galen into a spacious bedroom. With teeth gritted and tendons bulging in her neck, the other woman managed to heft the big brute onto a bed. Shaking now, she cut away his clothes to study his wounds. For some reason, he had stacks of paper underneath his shirt and leathers. Fox muttered curses about fool men endangering themselves for a quick roll in the hay and peeled away one blood-splattered sheet after another.

Close the distance. Help the man who helped you. Come on! But Legion stood rooted in place, quaking violently, clutching Sips to her chest, her mind whirling. Why had Galen saved her? There was no man more calculating or self-serving, so he must have a reason. Right? And yes, okay, his letters claimed he wanted her sexually, but physical desire wasn't a good enough reason to risk his life.

Although, to be fair, she could have died blissed-out the night Galen took her virginity. The sex had been hot and charged and good. Nothing like the travesty she'd suffered in hell.

Warning! Avoid! Memories of torture would put her in a fugue state.

Galen's agonized roar echoed from the walls, and she jolted, stumbling back. What if he... died?

She gulped. Once, she would have paid good money to witness his demise. Well, maybe not good money, but a pretty penny. Well, maybe not a pretty penny, either. Money bought jewels, and Legion loved jewels. Now? Their brief romp had prime real estate in her portfolio of wise decisions. Suddenly the idea of never seeing him again, never hearing his voice gutted her.

No. He would survive. He would!

Minutes later—an eternity—Galen mumbled questions about the realm's security.

Fox snapped, "Don't worry about an invasion. Worry about my temper. I told you not to leave the house. Someone put a contract on your life and—"

"Multiple someones," he replied, the words slurred. "A usual occurrence. Did you find out who?"

"Yes. You can thank Cronus 2.0. The bastard cloned himself before his death."

Galen heaved a sigh and slurred a response.

Legion thought he said: "Contact Sienna. And do not hurt my guest."

Even now, wracked with pain, he sought to secure her safety? A tear escaped, sliding down her cheek.

"Legion. Honey." Two names, two words—both innocent—and yet Fox had somehow turned them into curses. Her slate gray gaze shot to Legion and narrowed, though she still spoke directly to Galen. "Whatever her name, I don't trust her."

"You don't...trust anyone." His breaths turned shallow, more labored.

"Har har," Fox said, her tone as dry as the desert. "Why do you care about her? Tell me! Help me understand, because I want, I *need*, to kill her."

Yes, Galen. Tell us!

And maybe I should run before Fox makes good on her threat?

He replied, forcing Legion to translate: "For the first time in my existence, I have a purpose. I am fulfilled, satisfied, and content... when I get inside her."

Either he didn't mind making such a confession with Legion in the room, or he'd lost sight of everything but Fox and his pain.

"Gee. Thanks, Dad," Fox said. "Happy to know I've never added value to your life, and you care more about the girl with the magic—"

"Enough. Do not hurt... her, even with... words." He closed his eyes, his head lolling to the side.

Fox straightened and stalked closer to Legion. Concern darkened the other woman's eyes, while tension wove over her angular features.

The same tension plagued Legion, seeming to turn her limbs into boulders. She couldn't move. *Hurry! Before Fox strikes.* But Galen's friend...lover?... never attacked. She simply said, "If you enter this room, I'll make sure you leave it in a body bag." That said, she slammed the door in Legion's face.

Freedom beckoned. She could leave the home without having to fight her way out. Fox wouldn't know, or care. Galen wouldn't know, either, though he *would* care. But, in his condition, he could do nothing to stop her.

She expected a storm of relief.

Waiting…

Still waiting…

All she felt? Trepidation. What fresh horrors awaited her outside these walls?

Well, then. She would stay put.

Now relief stormed through her.

Sips scratched and bit her arm. Racoon speak for, *Put me down, you fool.*

"Okay, okay." After setting him on the floor, he scratched and bit her *leg,* just for giggles. As she protested, he ran away.

Rather than explore the house, Legion shut herself in the bedroom next to Galen's and unpacked her jewels. Precious treasures she considered a part of her family. All the while, the warrior's incredible scent teased her. Summer storms, dark spices, and masculine musk.

Maybe her stay here wouldn't be so bad.

* * * *

Days passed in a haze of sleepiness and anguish. Legion's nightmares returned full force. Sips the Traitor never visited the spacious chamber, leaving her alone, afraid, and betrayed. Why did she even miss that stupid raccoon?

Easy. He was a total dick, yes, but he was *her* dick.

Wait, that sounded wrong. Whatever! Her only comfort came from her jewels. *Stroke the precious.*

Galen bellowed a string of curses, and she flinched, her stomach flip-flopping. He roared *every* time he woke up. Aiding the warrior ceased being a simple desire—it became a complicated need. But how? As a former demon who'd specialized in maximizing her victim's pain, she had nothing to offer.

"Fox! Get your ass in here." His ragged voice wasn't as slurred as before. Had part of his tongue already grown back? "Make it stop."

Helplessness bombarded Legion. She had to think this through. To think it through, she'd have to first clear the debris from her head. Maybe she'd take a walk.

She peeked out her bedroom's only window, a sea of white greeting her. Clouds? Had Galen taken her to a level of the heavens, where Sent Ones hunted her kind for sport?

Okay, no walk. She shrank back and pressed her back against the wall. Inhale, exhale.

A self-help book had mentioned the merits of focusing on a monotonous activity, so she gave that a try and counted furniture. One: a four-poster bed with a feather-soft mattress and lovely pink canopy. Two: a vanity embedded with colorful gemstones. Three: a wardrobe overflowing with ball gowns. Four, five, six: jewelry boxes filled to the brim. Seven: a nightstand made of mother-of-pearl.

Her heart rate slowed, fear ebbing. This room seemed tailor-made for her, as if the designer had reached inside her brain and rooted through her preferences. Galen's doing?

The only flaw? The lack of books. In hell, reading was forbidden. But on one of Hades's rare visits to the cabin, he'd given her an iPod loaded with "how to" programs, and it hadn't taken long for the lessons to click. Now, Legion *loved* to read, to discover new worlds without ever leaving the safety of her home. No matter how savage, no matter how brutal, a romance novel hero never hurt his heroine, his icy exterior melting for her alone.

Am I Galen's *heroine?*

Did she want to be?

Clear your head and find out!

Fox's voice seeped through the walls, snagging her attention. "First you have to get better, but you're not getting better. *Why aren't you getting better, Galen?*"

Acid burned Legion's chest. Before, she'd worried Galen might die. Today, the possibility seemed more certain.

No. No! He would survive this, if only to save Legion from Fox. In books, the heroes never…or rarely died. Just depended on whether or not the author wanted Legion to track her down and complain! Although, Galen probably qualified as the villain, and villains *always* got axed.

Why not explore the house, clearing her head *and* mapping out an escape route, just in case?

Legion inched into the hallway, her feet as heavy as cinder blocks. Deep breath in, out. Good, that was good. A step forward, pause. Another step, pause. When she turned the corner and nothing bad happened, some of her tension drained. Steps lighter, she motored on, peeking into rooms and investigating the state-of-the-art appliances and expensive decor.

Galen had excellent taste, that was for sure. She recognized Qianlong and Ming Dynasty vases, exquisite Persian rugs, and priceless artwork collectors would probably commit terrible crimes to own. Artwork she vaguely remembered being reported *stolen* over the centuries.

Her host also possessed a wealth of technological marvels, reminiscent of the robotic birds he'd sent to the cabin. In a workroom, she found tables cluttered with tools, all kinds of metals, and different robots in varying stages of completion.

When she came upon an office, she nearly wept with joy. So. Many. Books. The mothership. Her new happy place. Maybe she could find a medical guide for immortals.

She searched the shelves, excitement morphing into disappointment. Nearly every tome dealt with war, torture, or overcoming a traumatic past.

What kind of traumas had he suffered in his long, long life? If his experiences had been anything like hers... An unexpected pang of sympathy speared her.

Focus! Maybe she would fire off a message to Aeron and Olivia to let them know she'd left the cabin, and ask if *they* knew how to save Galen's life.

And give the couple a chance to attack the warrior while he couldn't defend himself? No.

A book without a title caught her attention. She flipped through the pages, her eyes widening. A scrapbook about Gwendolyn the Fierce, Galen's daughter. The pages were filled with photographs of Gwen from the age of four-ish to adulthood.

He'd only recently found out about her, and he'd claimed to want nothing to do with her. Yet he'd dug so deeply into her past? Why would he hide—

"He's not getting better." The familiar voice spilled through the office, interrupting Legion's thoughts.

Jolting, she spun to face the threat. A fatigued Fox occupied the open doorway, her arms crossed over her chest, Sips purring as he wound around her feet like a cat.

Fear squeezed Legion's throat. Her heart thudded against her ribs, and nausea churned in her stomach. For a moment, her mind transported back to hell, when she'd been Lucifer's prisoner.

—a blindfold covered her eyes as a blade sliced into her torso. She screamed and fought to no avail. Demons cackled with glee—

—hot, fetid breath fanned her ear…fangs scraped between her breasts before sinking deep—

"No!" she shouted, struggling to breathe.

Fox gave her a withering glare.

Inhale, exhale. Tears burned her eyes. Legion hated being this girl. Once upon a time, she had faced every challenge with bravery and confidence. Nothing had frightened her.

"Calm down," Fox demanded. Taller than Legion by several inches and regal in a way few people could mimic, she didn't just command a room—she commanded all she surveyed. "I think Galen was poisoned while saving your worthless life."

A spark of anger torched the last vestiges of the past, a remnant of the old Legion snapping, "Or maybe you're just a crappy caregiver?"

"Wrong. I'm a *mediocre* caregiver. Now tell me what happened." Black lines branched from her eye sockets, a sign of fury, and a consequence of the demon she carried within.

"Around my house, there were wards designed to cause temporary brain bleeds and confusion, so that any attackers would forget me." Why hadn't Galen forgotten her? "As soon as we exited the cabin, Galen should have healed from that. As for his other injuries…I only saw an arrow pierce his wing. Everything else comes from battles he waged before he reached me." She nibbled on her lower lip. "If Lucifer sent the army, then Galen was poisoned."

Even saying the Destroyer's name left a foul taste in her mouth, but the suspicion of poison proved far worse. If only fear hadn't scrambled her brain, she would have realized it sooner!

She could have saved Galen days of anguish. If he'd reached the point of no return, reviving him would no longer be possible. Was she already too late?

"You still think Cronus is responsible?" she asked, hopeful.

"Yes. He probably used the same methods as the Prince of Darkness. Villains *do* learn from each other. So, tell me about the poison," Fox insisted. "Where can I find an antidote?"

"*La pire mort*. The worst death. The poison won't deactivate until Galen is dead. And there *isn't* an antidote."

Fox popped her jaw. Her hands fisted. "There has to be—"

"There isn't." Legion shook her head to punctuate her words, strands of hair slapping her cheeks. *La pire mort* provided an unescapable doom. "To save him, we'll have to kill him."

"No. Absolutely not. You're lying. You'd say anything to orchestrate his death."

"Then," she continued as if Fox hadn't spoken, "we'll have to revive him." There was no other way.

Anguish colored Fox's expression. "Say you're right. The moment he dies, the demons will leave him. When the demons leave him, there'll be a grand total of zero ways to revive him."

"Wrong. We can force the pair to stay put." Before Legion's semi-human transformation, Aeron had summoned her from the depths of hell and kept her trapped in a circle of salt and sugar. The mixture blistered demon flesh in ways fire could not. "Galen *will* revive." He must. "I'm doing this. Get on board or get out of my way."

Brave words from a cowardly girl. Still, she stormed past Fox, who—shocker—didn't try to stop her, and stomped down the hall. In the kitchen, she hunted for a bag of sugar and a container of salt. Only half-filled.

Oh, look. She'd thought *half-filled* rather than *half-empty*. That was new. Anyway. Half wouldn't form a complete circle around Galen, so, she gathered up the garlic salt, celery salt, and soy sauce as well.

"You planning to cook him for dinner after you murder him?" Fox asked.

"Dibs on his liver," she muttered, then marched down the hall a second time.

As she entered the bedroom, Fox stayed close. Sickness coated the air, stinging her nostrils. Galen writhed on a blood-soaked bed, his wings tangled with the sheets. He coughed and wheezed, crimson droplets spraying from his mouth.

Her chest constricted, guilt prickling the back of her neck once again. She'd let him languish in this condition, doing nothing.

She deserved to suffer like this.

After pouring a complete circle of salt and sugar around his body—yes!—she settled at his side, careful not to disrupt the granules. The heavy odor of garlic made her nose itch.

"Why sugar and salt?" Fox demanded. An obvious default setting.

"You know how some people are allergic to peanuts? Exactly like that, but totally different." She smoothed a trembling hand over Galen's brow, brushing back a lock of silver-blond hair. Torment etched his yellowed skin, rousing concern and compassion, overriding every other emotion. "I need a dagger."

The nausea returned with a vengeance. She hadn't held a weapon in a very long time. Had never wanted to hold one again. For Galen, though, she would do it. She owed him. But after this they would be even. 100%.

"I hope it goes without saying that I will remove your head if he doesn't revive," Fox grated.

She remembered a time when she would have looked at Fox, smiled, and ripped out the other woman's trachea. Now? She wilted like rose petals in scorching heat. "Threats aren't helping."

"I wasn't threatening." All rage and apprehension, Fox unsheathed a blade and slapped the hilt into Legion's upturned palm. "I was explaining the situation."

"I—I will kill him, and you will revive him. Deal?" Galen…dead…even for a few seconds…

"I have no experience with the latter."

Tension stole through her, her calm façade cracking. Why did she continue to care about this man? He wasn't misunderstood; he was bad to the bone. Over the centuries, he'd betrayed his friends, separated a multitude of mates, and harmed even more innocents. Men and women worldwide would rejoice at his death. She would be touted as a hero.

Legion still didn't know why he wanted her, either, or what he planned to do with her, but it couldn't be good, right? What if he used her against Aeron and the other Lords? What if he gave her back to Lucifer and collected the bounty on her head? What if he traded her— her life in exchange for a favor? What if he only wanted to punish her for once trying to kill him?

Fear flash-froze her blood. But…what if he'd meant what he'd written in those letters, and he yearned to spend more time with her? Longed to protect her. Because he craved her, body and soul, and hungered for her touch.

Could she touch him again, without remembering the terrible things she'd suffered soon afterward?

She didn't know, but thought she might maybe probably kinda sorta…want to find out.

A raspy moan slipped from his chapped lips—the death rattle. *Running out of time.*

"Let me help you, Galen," she whispered. "Let me ease your pain."

His lashes fluttered open, his gaze finding her. Recognition brightened in those ocean-water depths, followed by happiness. "You…worth it," he whispered back.

He found worth in her? *Her? She* had put the happiness in his eyes? Her chest clenched. Maybe he *did* crave her.

"I'm so sorry," she told him. "For everything I've done…and will do." With a fresh stream of hot tears scorching her cheeks, she placed the tip of the dagger at his heart. Deep breath in…

The happiness vanished. "You…betray?"

CLENCH. "Please understand. There's no other way to make you better."

He reached up to clasp her wrist, his grip loose, weak.

"I'm so sorry," she repeated, raw and ragged. *Do it!*

Exhaling, she pushed the blade deep and twisted. He used his final breath to curse her. His head lolled to the side, his eyes staring somewhere beyond her, as if he didn't want her face to be the last thing he saw.

Galen the Magnificent died exactly as he'd lived: a heartbreaker.

The demons rose from his body, two dark clouds with skeletal faces and neon red eyes. Pure, undiluted hatred emanated from the pair, and she stumbled back.

When the demons scented the salt and sugar, they dove back into Galen to hide.

"Hurry, hurry." Every second mattered.

Fox swooped in to get to work.

"Heal him." This time, Legion was the one to issue a demand. "Heal him *now*." Or else.

Chapter Five

Galen awoke with a roar of denial brewing at the back of his throat. After centuries of training, he had the wherewithal to cut off the sound before it escaped. No need to alert a nearby foe that he was up and ready to kick ass.

He jolted upright and flared his wings, preparing for flight. A lance of pain heralded a wave of dizziness and hazy vision. Flight proved impossible, and also unnecessary. He thought he might be in his bedroom. The one next to the chamber he'd prepared for Legion's stay. As he eased back down, he recognized the softness of the mattress and comforter.

Aches and pains plagued his battered body, his muscles screaming in protest. His lungs struggled to inflate, as if the organs had been dipped in wet cement.

What the hell had happened to him? And why did his room smell like a chicken wing buffet?

He blinked rapidly, a wealth of memories taking shape in his head. Multiple battles and injuries. Legion's rescue. Losing his tongue and tooth—both had grown back. Fox. A portal home. A dagger to the heart?

He *did* have a slightly warped heartbeat. Frowning, he scrubbed a hand over his sternum. No wound.

When his vision cleared, he gave the room a cursory scan. Yep. His. Except for the blood-soaked dagger resting on the nightstand, nothing had changed since his last visit.

That dagger solidified his suspicion. He had been stabbed. Who would dare—

The memory crystalized, and he growled. *Legion* had wielded the weapon.

The object of his obsession had tried to kill him. Again! She had apologized and cried, but she hadn't stopped driving that dagger into his heart.

Darkness had enveloped his mind, so much darkness, and he'd seemed to fall, fall into an endless abyss. Then lights had flashed and Fox had screamed from far away. *Come back to me, or I'll kill Legion. I swear I will.*

He remembered what felt like a hammer beating on his chest. Remembered Legion begging Fox to hurry and revive him.

There's no other way to make you better. I'm sorry.

As Legion's final words drifted through his head, his anger eased. In her tone, he detected genuine remorse, agony, and determination. So the girl who usually vomited at the sight of blood had killed him, yes, but she hadn't wanted him to stay dead.

Ding, ding, ding. Another detail surfaced. Fox had jabbered about his death deactivating some kind of poison. An interesting development. If Legion had truly reviled him, she would have let him die for real, forever. But she hadn't.

Hope bloomed bright, shiny, and exquisite. She'd gone to a lot of trouble to save him. Because she *cared* about him.

Or because False Hope had made her want something from him?

You are the reason I can't have nice things, he spat at the fiend.

Gleeful laughter echoed, and yeah, Galen wanted to punch a hole in his skull.

Where had Legion gone? Now that he was on the mend, they needed to chat about the present and the future.

A strangled sound assailed his ears. He went still and quiet, casting his gaze around the room a second time. There, behind the headboard, Legion slept curled up on a recliner.

Primitive satisfaction rocked him. A sensation he'd never before enjoyed. His woman was here, within reach, her wildflower scent tantalizing him. *Let this never end.*

The scabs in his shoulder pulled as he reached for the cell phone on his nightstand. He teed up Aeron's number and texted: **Just a head's up. I've got my girl. She's well thanks to me. Hades would have let her get jacked. You're welcome.**

Aeron's response came in minutes: **H told me you saved her. For that, you do have my thanks. But you're going to have internal** body bling if you don't return her to me ASAP.

Galen: **Give me a minute to find the fucks I give…**

Galen: **Still searching…**

Galen: **Sorry. Can't find a single one.**

Aeron: **I love her, and I want what's best for her, even if I must pay for her happiness w/ my life. Can you say the same?**

Galen responded with a gif he'd made for situations like this. In it, he made a lewd hand gesture while the words "Look what I gave your mother last night" flashed in the center.

Then he typed: **Listen, Dr. Usuc Atfilosofee. I didn't see you braving H's wards to help L escape that bloodthirsty army. (Drop mic.) (Pick mic back up.) She's safe, ok. And I CAN say the same. I DID protect her with my life. So be a good daddy and let your daughter spread my wings. Over and out, mo-fo.**

He returned the cell phone to the nightstand.

Legion gave a violent shake of her head and released another choking sound. "No. Please, no."

He could imagine what images plagued her nightmares.

Uncaring about the flare of pain, he leaped off the bed to crouch in front of her chair. He lightly caressed her jaw, then lifted her hand to his face, holding her palm against his cheek. "I'm here, sugar." His raw throat turned the words to smoke.

A few months ago, Galen had made a deal with Hades. Every time Galen completed a task for the underworld's top dog, he earned a reward. All he'd wanted? The demons who'd hurt Legion. He'd tortured and killed every one of the bastards but Lucifer.

"No. Please, no. Don't!" Eyes rolling behind her lids, Legion panted and groaned. Every few seconds, her fingers twitched, as if she tried to deflect a blow. "No!"

He ground his teeth. One day, one day soon, this beauty would rest in the comfort and security of his arms. Fear would lose its hold on her, and contentment would become her constant companion. *I'll make sure of it.*

"I won't let anything happen to you," he vowed. "Not now, not ever."

She melted into the chair, a soft sigh leaving her. Pride suffused him. For once, he'd comforted rather than frightened her.

Though he yearned to linger, he returned to the bed, lest he terrify her when she awoke.

Before he resettled, he cast her a final glance, his heart thudding. *My downfall is exquisite. Flawless even.* She wore a black tank top and gray sweat pants rolled at the waist and ankles. Adorable, yes, but he missed the prom dress. The long length of her honey-blonde hair cascaded over one delicate shoulder. Roses painted her cheeks, exactly where he'd caressed her. Jewels adorned her: diamonds around her neck, rubies and sapphires around her wrists, rings on every finger.

Maybe her dreams had nothing to do with her past. Maybe she worried for Galen? The idea pleased him. Unless he had False Hope to thank? The demon enjoyed building him up, just to tear him down. The higher his hopes, the harder he crashed. Of course, at his lowest, Jealousy would whisper sweet nothings in his ear. *You deserve so much more. Take it!*

Then False Hope would swoop in to build Galen back up. *Once you remove the obstacles in your path, you'll be so happy.*

As soon as Galen overreached, and he always overreached, he would lose something he valued. The fiends would cackle with glee, and the process would start all over again.

Galen would give anything to extract the pair. But, when an immortal bonded with a person, place or thing, whether willingly or unwillingly, he tied his life-force to it. One could not survive without the other.

The only upside to Galen's companions—they hurt his enemies just as thoroughly as they hurt him.

The thought of Legion being harmed in such a way…

Stiff as a board, he said, "Wake up, beautiful."

She obeyed with the finesse of a freight train, erupting out of the chair while throwing a punch. Her whiskey-colored gaze glittered with terror as she scanned the room, her pupils the size of saucers. When she spotted him, the terror gave way to relief. After she gave him a once-over, the relief gave way to awareness.

Awareness? Or more wishful thinking on his part? He'd wanted this woman for so long.

No, it *must* be genuine. The air between them heated, as sultry as a stormy summer night.

His cells sizzled, struck by lightning bolts of desire.

"You're alive," she rasped.

The pessimistic side of him reared up. "Are you disappointed?"

"After working with Fox to bring you back from the dead? No."

"I remember your last words." In a falsetto, he said, "*Oh, Galen, my gorgeous lover boy, there's no other way to make you better. You must live, for I will perish without you.*"

She took the bait, bristling. "I did *not* call you a lover boy."

But you will. Soon. "Did you think it? You can tell me. I'll keep your secret."

Her cheeks flushed, revving his desire another notch. How hot did her skin burn? "What you did, you did to help me. I get it," he said. "But I'm not happy that you gambled with my future. When a demon-possessed immortal kicks it, his spirit ends up in a prison realm." Galen had spent too much time in prison already.

Most recently, the Cronus clone had sheared off his wings and caged him alongside an immortal named Keeleykael, AKA The Red Queen, one of the strongest beings in history, with a megaton of superpowers.

Galen respected and admired Keeley. He even loved her. Shockingly, their friendship persevered even after she hooked up with Torin, keeper of Disease.

An invisible knife twisted in Galen's chest. Once, Torin had been his best friend. If the guy couldn't forgive a massive betrayal of his trust and a few hundred measly murder attempts, he didn't deserve to have Galen in his life.

"How are you feeling?" Legion moved to the side of the bed, swept sugar and salt granules to the floor, and eased down. Laser focused, she reached out, clearly intending to press her hand against his forehead. At the last second, she stiffened and dropped her arm to her side without making contact.

He *ached* for contact with her. Why pull back? What did she fear most about him? And how could he help her overcome it?

If the fear had roots in intimacy, he knew of only one way to help. Initiate contact so often the act became as automatic as breathing.

Tough job, but he would find a way to push through.

Step one: *give her a reason to touch him—or an excuse.*

Galen sagged against his pillows, as if strength had deserted him. "I'm feeling feverish." Truth. His cells only sizzled hotter, and only Legion had the power to cool him down... *after* she'd burned him alive with passion.

"Any other symptoms of infection?" she asked, reaching out...Yes! This time, she pressed her hand against his forehead. A sense of triumph flared.

Step two: *fight a smile when you succeed.*

He leaned into her touch, luxuriating in her soft as velvet, warm as freshly tapped molasses skin.

Step three: *enjoy.*

How sweet would she taste?

"Good news. You're hot, but not *too* hot." Her gaze traveled over him. In an instant, a choked noise rose from her; she jumped to her feet and spun around, severing contact.

He swallowed a curse and gave himself a once-over, wondering what had caused such a vehement reaction. Well. *Hello, hard-on. How I've missed you.* Since taking Legion's virginity, being with other women had proven impossible. His body wanted her, and only her. Now, having her nearby...

He *needed* sex.

"Why did you save me?" she asked, changing the subject. "And don't say you just wanted to sleep with me. Your desire is kind of obvious. I want the real reason."

"*Kind of* obvious? Darling, there's nothing *kind of* about my erection."

Her cheeks pinkened. "There must be more to it than that. And I'm not talking about your erection!"

The show of spirit activated a battle cry inside Galen's head: *More!*

Give someone the truth, the whole truth, and nothing but the truth? Usually he refused. When you spoke your truths aloud, you revealed secret shames, hidden desires, and masked vulnerabilities. An inadvertent consequence, but a consequence all the same. Why give someone unnecessary power over you? But this was Legion. The exception to his every rule, apparently.

"To understand why I did what I did," he said, "you need a little background."

"I'm listening."

"Like all former soldiers in Zeus's army, I was created fully formed. Unlike most of the others, I experienced an immediate desire to lead, to conquer, to own *everything* I surveyed. The desire has only grown stronger over the centuries." Every time he'd won a battle, Fate itself seemed to say: *You are meant to rule.*

"So...you want me to co-own the world with you?" she asked, her brow furrowed.

Yes. No. He wanted to co-own her pleasure. And he would. But that particular truth would only frighten her.

"When you were being tortured in hell," he said, proceeding with caution, "I went after you. I didn't know the awfulness of the deeds being done to you, I just knew part of me wanted to strike at you the way you'd struck at me while the other part of me wanted you back in my bed. But I let a personal vendetta against someone else derail my plans. A fact I will forever regret. So when I discovered an army marched for your cabin, nothing and no one could stop me from getting to you. Now," he added with a sigh, "I want a chance to help you heal, Leg—Honey. I *need* to help you."

She didn't bolt. A good sign. "You may call me Legion," she whispered. "It's fine."

No, it wasn't. Her name, her choice. He'd been an ass to insist otherwise. "How about I call you…Leila," he said, and nodded, enamored of the syllables as they rolled from his tongue.

She frowned. "Leila?"

"L-E from Legion, paired with I-L-A."

"Ila. *Dark beauty* in the old language." The corners of her mouth twitched, the sight nearly his undoing. "Yes! I love, love, love it."

Could a male spontaneously orgasm? That almost smile really lit the fuse on his rocket.

"Why did *you* save *me*?" he asked, his head tilting to the side. And what did her letters say?

The letters! Some of the papers had gotten soaked with blood. Surely a few remained legible. Where had Fox left them? Next time he rolled solo, he would go hunting.

Slowly, hands wringing together, Legion said, "I saved you because…I owed you."

Duty, then. Disappointment blistered him with the heat of a thousand suns, but not by word or deed did he reveal it. In fact, pride glued on a couldn't-care-less expression. Unfortunately, pride used weak glue.

"And because you intrigue me," she added, her voice soft. "And because I remembered how good it felt to be with you. And because I'm tired of being afraid every second of every day. And because I don't know how to change, or how to protect myself. Maybe you could…I don't know…teach me? *Maybe*," she reiterated.

As his heart raced, False Hope whispered poison. *The more time you spend with her, the more she'll learn about you, and the more she'll hate you.*

The opposite of hope? Fear. Once again, the demon's greatest weapon.

Galen bit his tongue until he tasted blood. "Yes," he said. "I will teach you."

Oblivious to his inner turmoil, Legion—Leila—said, "You told Fox that Sienna will protect you. I'm assuming you spoke of Sienna Blackstone, keeper of Wrath, wife to Paris, and current queen of the Titans."

"The very one."

"*How?*"

He understood the question—how had he garnered such a promise. "A while back, she and the Lords were desperate to find Pandora's box." After they'd opened it all those centuries ago, it had vanished. No big deal, except the box supposedly had the power to kill every demon-possessed immortal in the world. "Four artifacts were needed to find it. I had one, and we traded. The artifact for two years of protection."

The Lords had gotten the better end of the bargain, no doubt about it. They'd eventually found the box. So far, Sienna had done shit for Galen.

Legion—damn it, Leila—surprised him by asking, "Since we're talking about the infamous box, why did you betray your friends and tell Zeus they planned to steal it?"

"Many reasons," he grated, hating this subject. "Why are you so curious?" Already looking for a reason to ditch him and his lessons?

She ignored his question. "Name three reasons for doing what you did."

He narrowed his eyes. "Why?"

"I'm, well…" She hiked her shoulders in a shrug, doing her best to appear casual. "I'm interviewing you for the position of my helper."

Considering how much he wanted the job, he opted for honesty yet again. "One, Lucien and Sabin were leaders of Zeus's Elite Guard and I hoped they'd get fired. Two, I liked Pandora, and I didn't want her executed if the steal-and-open plan succeeded. Three, I tried to talk to the guys about my reservations, but they ignored me, so I decided they deserved to fail."

"So…out of spite?"

"Yes," he admitted.

Silence stretched between them, tense and oppressive, her thoughts clearly spinning. He opened his mouth to give her the hard sell, thought better of it, and said nothing. He wanted Leila to crave the real Galen, not some fake veneer.

Besides, if he said anything more, he might push her away rather than urge her closer. His fragile flower had to be handled with care. But waiting had never been easy for Galen. When he wanted something, he *wanted* it. And Leila…he wanted her more than he'd ever wanted anyone else.

"What will we do if Cronus or Lucifer finds us?" she asked.

"They won't. You're safe here. No one knows I own this realm, and no one can enter without portaling in. Few immortals wield the magic needed to portal, and neither bastard has a Gatekeeper on staff." Not even Hades had one, though rumors suggested Hades's son William possessed the ability to a limited degree.

Finally, Leila nodded. "I hate to bargain, but I know of no other way to do this. You will protect me, and help me overcome my fears, *all* my fears, moving at a pace I find comfortable, and I will…" She nibbled on her bottom lip, an obvious habit. "What do you want from me in return?"

No need to ponder. "You. I will devour every inch of you, if ever you give me permission," he said, his voice husky with longing. "For now, we'll start with a dinner date."

Chapter Six

After Leila returned to her bedroom, Galen texted Fox a set of instructions. Then he found and read the letters Leila had written but never sent. As he'd hoped, some had remained legible.

Her replies ran the gamut, everything from "leave me alone" to "never stop wanting me" to "I'd never known true satisfaction until our interlude in the bar. In hell, I was a piece of property, passed from one abuser to another. I meant nothing. I WAS nothing. To you, I think I mattered."

The words blurred at that point. Because he'd gotten dust in his eyes.

He felt the same way about her. He might not matter to her—yet—but the moment he'd come inside her was the one and only time he'd experienced true satisfaction. For the first time in his life, something other than a ravenous hunger for power had controlled him. Actually, even that hunger had been momentarily assuaged. She'd consumed his thoughts and enslaved his body.

In her letters, Leila also mentioned that she wished she'd stayed with him after they'd had sex, and wondered what her life would have been like if she'd chosen a different path.

He couldn't change the past for her, but he could do everything possible to ensure he left her in better condition than he'd found her…and no other man ever had a chance to compare.

Another man…touching my woman…

I'll kill him.

Galen showered, brushed his teeth about a thousand times, and dressed for the coming dinner date with great care. All the while, he trembled with eagerness. *Not* nervousness. Nope. Not him. He didn't do nervous.

He checked his reflection in the full-length mirror to search for flaws. Not a single one. The dark pin-striped suit made from the finest silk money could buy had cutouts for his wings, and the white button-up molded to his *significant* muscle mass. *Dayum.* He looked so good he had a crush on *himself.* His pale hair appeared wind-blown, but also perfect. Dare he mention the sparkle in his electric blues?

Leila's reservations would melt like ice cream on a hot summer's day. And so would her panties.

Unless she's using you as a substitute for Aeron.

He stiffened. Clearly, False Hope and Jealousy planned to ruin his evening. Well, too bad, so sad. *Nothing* could ruin this. Except for a long list of emotional landmines, of course. His past. His present. His future. His attitude. Going too fast. Going too slow. Basically—everything about him.

The trembling worsened. Because he was even more eager, *not* even more nervous.

He would be meeting Leila in the kitchen in T-minus fifty-nine minutes, twenty-eight seconds, and he would romance the hell out of her.

So he hadn't been on a date in…ever. So what? He excelled at everything.

Yes, you do, False Hope said. *Most of all, you excel at failure.*

Inhale. Exhale. Ignore the fiend. In the past, if Galen had wanted a woman he'd either A) paid for a few hours of her time or B) flirted, had sex, then blazed a path to the nearest exit. He'd never had more than a one-night stand. Why build a life the demons would one day destroy?

Besides, Galen had trust issues. And rightly so. Welcoming a lover into his home would only end one of three ways. An attack while he was distracted by pleasure—a ploy he'd often used against his foes. An ambush at a later date. His personal information leaked to others. No, thanks.

Going to a female's place had been out of the question, too. He had too many enemies willing to use women as bait.

Distraction killed as surely as a blade.

But again, Leila proved to be an exception to his every rule.

"I finally got to speak with Sienna." Fox's voice sounded behind him.

He turned on the heels of his expensive Italian loafers, one brow quirked. "And?"

She stood in front of the door, Sips at her feet. The trash panda had taken a liking to her. "She told me you're alive today only because she's handled some of the contracts on your life. She asked that you lay low, and mentioned she'll help Aeron skin you alive if you harm Legion."

What if Aeron decides he wants Leila as his sidepiece? Will she go running back to him?

You can't *win her affections. Why try?*

Jealousy, attempting to shift his focus. False Hope, attempting to stop him before he even started.

He stiffened. *Ignore. Them.* "Did you do as I requested and—"

"Google the best questions to ask on a first date? Yes," she interjected, waving a handful of notecards.

"And did you—"

"Kidnap a chef who specializes in Legion's preferred cuisine? Yes, again."

"And—"

"Buy Legion a cell phone?" She tossed the device his way. "Yes."

Excellent. Like him, Leila had never really been on a date. Galen wanted to set the bar high with her favorite foods and gifts.

Fox crossed the distance, stopping in front of him to straighten his tie. "The meal is ready. I took the chef home and ensured he forever doubts what he saw and heard."

One of Distrust's only perks—instilling self-doubt in others. Few people knew how to recognize the fiend's whispers.

Sips followed Fox and wound around her ankles. Something about the creature set off alarms in Galen's head. His gaze, maybe. Far too direct.

"Is your new pet a shifter?" he asked.

"No. He's a spy. Hades can link with him at any time. But Sips tells me whenever the king is at the wheel."

"Oh, so you speak raccoon now?"

"Like it's hard?" She smirked and fluffed her hair. "Be glad I learned. Sips is the one who told me all of your girlfriend's beloved culinary delights."

Girlfriend. A word he would never tire of hearing. "Thank you for aiding me."

"I have a feeling you won't be so grateful when you taste the gourmet circus cuisine." She shuddered. "At first, Sips told me she liked fried squirrel on a stick. After I threatened to neuter him, he fessed up to the truth, which is just as horrifying."

Were they talking about circus peanuts and popcorn? His palate wept.

"Just…hurry up and nail the girl so your obsession with her will fade, and we can get back to our world domination agenda." She opened her mouth to say more, frowned, then shook her head.

Did the demon of Distrust attempt to poison her thoughts against Leila? Or Galen?

He'd known the possibility existed before he'd captured the fiend, but he'd considered the risk worth the reward.

Galen cupped one side of her face and pressed a soft kiss into the other. "We have an eternity to advance our world domination agenda. For the next week—month—maybe the next year, let's focus on our personal shit." Was a year long enough, though? "Go, get lost for a while. Enjoy an evening of debauchery anywhere but here."

"I love you, too," she grumbled.

"I love you, yes. With all my heart. But you are a cock-block. You always cramp my style."

"You mean your *slay now, question later* style?"

"Close. *Lay* now, question later."

She pretended to gag. "You might not want me nearby, but you need me. Legion's bite is still venomous. If she attacks—"

"Let me stop you there. Whatever happens, you aren't to harm Leila—Legion. Tell me you understand this."

"But—"

"I don't care if you come back and find my severed limbs roasting on a spit. She's off limits to you. Say it."

Her eyes narrowed, but she grated, "Legion is off limits to me."

"Good girl." He patted Fox's cheek in approval, accepted the notecards, and strode out of the room, ready to begin Leila's seduction…

* * * *

Shocked to the bone, Legion performed a slow-mo 360. Galen's kitchen had been transformed into an Arabian Nights paradise. Flickering candles filled the entire room. Multi-colored scarves cascaded from the ceiling, intermixing with strings of beads. A coffee table had replaced the kitchen table, jewel-toned pillows acting as chairs. Covered platters dominated the table's surface, a gem-encrusted genie lamp the centerpiece.

Your wish is my command...

The scent of corn dogs, chili cheese fries, and cotton candy saturated the air, and her mouth watered.

As Galen stepped past a sheer purple curtain, electric pulses awakened every nerve in her body.

He looked her over. "You are stunning, Leila."

His husky timbre sent shivers rushing down her spine. And when he looked her over a second time, taking in the frilly dress with a cinched-in waist and mid-thigh tulle skirt paired with ballet flats, his irises heated—and so did her blood.

Galen wore a dark, perfectly tailored suit, the polished veneer only enhancing the savagery of his soul. Awareness of him eclipsed her fears, and it was nice. Better than nice. Wonderful! For a moment, she felt like the old Legion again.

"I'm guessing I am stunning, too?" he prompted.

Did she detect a thrum of uncertainty? How *adorable*. The saucy, ultra-confident Galen cared about her opinion. Meaning she had power over him. How delicious.

"You are," she admitted. "I think you've hijacked my thoughts." And she was glad for it. Once, she'd made a deal with the devil because she'd dreamed of falling in love, being loved in return, and discovering why humans were so obsessed with getting naked and rolling around in bed. Here, now, she realized a part of her still yearned for those things, despite everything that had happened.

Fear had put her life on pause long enough. She *deserved* pleasure.

If she wanted better, she had to fight for it. Had she picked the right man for the job, though? Someone who would be patient with her, who would ease her back to life, and give as much as he took?

Time would reveal the truth, one way or another, but her hopes were high. Galen was strong. He would cross any line to get what he wanted, and for some reason, what he wanted most was a chance to keep her safe.

Unless he decided to bed her, even if she said no.

Sickness churned in her stomach. She would never be able to fight him off. Her body might appeal to males, but it was too frail, too weak.

"Whatever you're thinking," Galen grated, "stop. Please. False

Hope is gleeful." He clasped her hand, stopping her from continuing to stroke the diamond choker around her neck.

"I don't understand. My thoughts aren't hopeful. They're dark."

He kissed her wrist, his lips brushing the spot where her pulse hammered. The action surprised her and caused her brain to short-circuit. "Dark, as in fearful?" When she nodded, he added, "Fear is a type of hope. An expectation of the worst possible outcome."

Yes, of course. *Should have realized.* Having grown up in hell, she had firsthand experience with demon trickery. The best way to combat False Hope? Truth.

If Galen had wanted to hurt her, he'd had multiple opportunities. In return for saving her life, he could have asked for anything, even sex. When he'd woken up and realized she'd driven a blade through his heart, he hadn't jumped to conclusions and punished her. He'd thought things through.

Fear? Suddenly, she had none, the truth freeing her from its shackles.

Galen must have sensed the change in her. He grinned, seduction incarnate, and waved to the table. "Sit. Please."

Helpless to resist, she eased onto a pillow at one side of the coffee table. He selected a pillow directly across from her, his body heat and scent quickly enveloping her, more intense than usual.

He filled a plate with food, handed it to her, then filled another, only cringing twice.

"You aren't a fan of corndogs, I take it," she said. "Are you too sophisticated?"

"You mean am I someone who prefers his food not to go in one end and spew out the other? One hundred percent yes."

"Did you just reference…you did, you really did." She laughed with abandon.

Fascination lit his eyes, and she quieted. Her cheeks heated.

"Well," she said, and cleared her throat. "We have nothing in common taste-wise."

He slanted his head to the side. "And things in common is important to you?"

"According to the self-help books I've read, similar likes and dislikes are touted as 'important,' yes, but only if you want to make your relationship work."

I'm thinking in terms of a relationship? Already?

Well, why not? Galen was the only person who excited her, in addition to terrifying her.

The likelihood that he would betray her at some point, in some way? High. Once, he'd been friends with the Lords. Then he'd ensured they got caught with their hands in the cookie jar. Or rather, Pandora's box. For centuries, he'd warred with his former friends, had even murdered one. Baden, former Keeper of Distrust.

Sure, Galen and the Lords had since made up. But she knew he wouldn't hesitate to take one out if it meant saving his own life. No one self-preserved like Galen. Would he willingly take out *Legion* to serve his cause? Whatever his cause happened to be.

Ugh. Had False Hope attacked her thoughts again?

Galen reached over to ghost his knuckles along her jaw, cajoling her from her thoughts. "Tell what troubles you. Let me help ease you."

"I'm wondering if I can ever trust you," she admitted softly. She'd demanded the truth from him, so she would offer the same in return.

His lips pressed into a thin line. "I've changed. I've learned the value of genuine friendship, and I will die to protect the people I consider mine."

What do you consider me? No, no. She wouldn't ask.

Picking up the conversation where they'd left off, he said, "We *are* in a relationship—your words, not mine, no take-backs—and we do have things in common. We both have a dark, seedy past. We have dreams for a better future. And let's not forget our sexual desires. We both enjoy climaxing."

Maybe he was right. Maybe he'd changed. Maybe they had things in common, and they could make something work. But sexual desire...

The blood rushed out of her head, her ears ringing. Knowing she deserved pleasure and actually remaining calm while experiencing it proved to be two different animals.

He reached for her once again, and this time she flinched. She'd started something, and now she wasn't sure she could ever finish.

He stilled, then dropped his hand to his side. The fascination she'd loved seeing in his eyes morphed into disappointment.

"I'm sorry," she whispered. "I didn't mean—"

"No, you did nothing wrong," he interjected. "I want you. I want you badly. And I think you want me, too. You wouldn't be here otherwise. But you never have to worry that I'll push you for sex. Your pleasure matters to me, and if you aren't ready, you won't experience pleasure. Besides, I can't bed you until I'm certain you're not going to try to kill me."

Ouch. Another flinch.

He added, "Too soon to joke about?"

"Forever might be too soon." She heaved a sigh. "Galen, I don't know if I'll ever be able to give myself...to do..."

"Do you remember our first time?" he asked.

As if she could ever forget. She had stomped right up to him and said, "I don't want to wed you, and I don't want to have your babies. We're gonna have sex, and you're gonna like it."

He'd replied, "Let me get this straight. We're going to the bathroom, and I'm going to fuck you, and you don't even care to know my name?"

"I'd actually prefer it if you'd keep your stupid mouth closed," she'd told him.

"Well, well. You might just be my soulmate," he'd replied.

"Yes," she said now. "I do."

"Good. Just making sure. As for our different palates—" He held up a French fry. "—food is of little consequence. The company you keep matters more."

He wasn't wrong. She liked what she liked, and he liked what he liked. As long as they had fun together, the cuisine wasn't important.

Legion ate with gusto, and oh, the flavors exploded on her tongue. Galen watched her, seemingly fascinated again, maybe even mesmerized...and ravenous. When she licked cotton candy from her lips, his pupils spilled over his irises, like ink spreading over the surface of an ocean.

He might not like the food, but he definitely enjoyed the sight of her eating it.

New shivers danced over her spine, surprising her. Tingles in her breasts followed. Between her legs, she ached.

Well. No wonder he'd reminded her of their first time. The memory had sensitized certain parts of her body.

He cleared his throat and muttered, "I have a present for you."

"A present? For me?" She bounced in her seat. "Gimme!"

He reached into his pocket and withdrew a cell phone. "This is fully loaded with fashion apps, and has my number programmed into the contact list. It will work anywhere, any time."

Hugging the phone to her chest, she said, "Thank you, Galen. I love it."

Expression dazed, he offered a nod of acceptance. "Time for a distraction. I mean, a conversation starter." One of his big, beautiful hands reached out and lifted a card from the stack next to the lamp. Reading aloud, he said, "If you were a shape, which one would you be?" He narrowed his eyes and scowled. "You've got to be kidding me."

"Probably a square?" she began.

Motions jerky, he lifted another card. "Which celebrity name is on your hall pass?" Deeper scowl. Another card. "If you were an X-rated Hallmark-type movie, what would you be titled?"

"Give me a chance to answer," she said, exasperated. "Hmm. Let's see. My title would be…"

"You don't have to respond," he grumbled.

"Oh! I know! My title would be *I'll Be Evil For Christmas*. What about you?"

The corners of his mouth twitched. "*A Royal Christmas Fuck Up*." With a sigh, he dropped the cards. "Forget the distraction—I mean the conversation starters."

He'd been so nervous about dating her, he'd needed help with things to talk about? More than adorable—heartwarming. She smiled. A full-blown one. Then she laughed again, her entire body shaking. Then *he* was laughing, and it was such a perfect moment of merriment and communion. A moment she'd never thought to experience with anyone ever again. Just like desire.

You can have a future with this man…

Such a beautiful thought. So hopeful. But the food she'd eaten turned to lead inside her stomach, her amusement dying fast. Was the thought *too* hopeful, mayhap? Like *False Hope* hopeful, setting her up for a terrible fall?

Humans had always likened "love" to falling. *I'm falling in love with you*. Blah, blah, blah. But falling wasn't fun, or welcome. When you hit, you hit hard. Sometimes different parts of you shattered. Like the ability to trust, or the wherewithal to fight for happiness.

Legion wasn't sure she could crawl away from another fall, much less survive it.

"So," she croaked, pulling at the collar of her dress. "You said we would start our new relationship with a dinner date."

He blinked, as if curious where she was headed. "I did."

"What's next, then?"

His gaze held hers and heated another thousand degrees. Only when she squirmed in her seat did he say, "For one month, we're going to hardcore court each other. We will write love notes—and actually deliver them. We'll have dinner together every night, smile and flirt. We will give each other more gifts."

Courted. *Her.* As if she was someone special. The thought made her a little giddy. "But couples have sex. I wasn't exaggerating before. I don't know if I can."

"You misunderstand. We're only pretending to be a couple, so we can take our relationship for a test drive. After we've gotten a taste of commitment, we'll decide if we want to try for real."

That wasn't a terrible idea. Excitement actually bubbled up. "Quick question. Since I don't have any money, and I don't want to leave the house to go shopping, are you good with homemade gifts? Like, I could paint a breathtaking mural on one of your walls or something."

"I enjoy murals with naked females lounging inside massive seashells. Give the robo-birds a list of all the paints and supplies you'll need, and they'll fetch everything."

"Oh, that'll be easy. I'll need one rolling brush and a can of pink paint."

His dark brows knit together. "Your mural will consist of a single color?"

"I'll call it...cloudless pink sky," she said, waving her hand for extra flair.

Eyes twinkling, he said, "How about *I* paint *you* a mural? When I lived in the heavens, I painted as a hobby. I'm quite good. I'll create a massacre of our enemies on one side of the wall, and a celebration ball on the other side. We'll call one Leila's Darkness and the other Leila's Light."

Our enemies, he'd said, not just hers. As if they were already a couple. A team. "I want both murals more than anything else in the world. Give them to me!" Uh-oh. Her demon side was showing.

"The murals will be my first gift to you, then." He lifted her hand and kissed her knuckles. "I'll also bring Aeron here for a reunion."

She shook her head. "I'm not ready to see Aeron."

"Why?"

"I just...part of me resents him, I guess."

He leaped to his feet, all menace and aggression. "This part of you resents him for choosing Olivia? Does that part of you want to be with him?"

"No, not at all," she replied, wondering why she wasn't afraid. "I had what humans call dog love."

Some of his tension faded. "You mean puppy love?" He returned to the pillow.

"A puppy is a dog, yes? Plus, every time I see his face, I remember his horror when he rescued me, which makes me remember what was done to me, which makes me hate myself."

"Then no Aeron." His touch feather-light, Galen caressed her jawline. He did it so swiftly she had no time to process his intention, only experienced the lovely result. "If ever you hate yourself, tell me. I will like you enough for both of us."

The things this darling man said…the things he did… the gifts he gave.

Wait. Darling? *Galen? What's happening to me?* Speaking of the gifts he gave. "I never thanked you properly for the demon heads. I loved them, and I promise I'll never ever re-gift."

He gave her the barest hint of a smile. "Now, all of the immortal world knows. Hurt Leila, and die extra bad."

Sweetest. Words. Ever. "Last time I saw you, you were living with the Lords. You were almost on friendly terms."

"We aren't the best of friends, but we aren't the worst of enemies, either. I value their lives." Pause. "I value yours more."

He really did. He valued her. Her! He had every reason to hate her, but he continued to woo her. The effort he'd already taken with her, with no promise of a reward… He was *trying*, doing everything in his power to become what she needed. With his every action, he proved his words and his intent a little more.

In that moment, something infinitely tender came over Legion. She threw herself against him, wrapping her arms around his shoulders. "I'm happy I met you, Galen, and I'm even happier you survived meeting me."

Chapter Seven

Hardcore courting rocked.

For the first time in his life, Galen forgot the rest of the world. War in the underworld—who cared? World domination—maybe later.

Pleasure—never-ending.

As Leila watched, he swirled two fingers in the tin of paint, blending colors. She moaned, and he had to hide a smile.

"Are you pained, my sweet?" he asked, playing the innocent. A role he'd perfected.

"No. Just thinking." She licked her lips. "You should paint the demons without clothes, and snare their genitals in claw-traps. You know, to give the mural a little spice."

Wiping his fingers on his bare chest to draw her gaze there, he stepped closer to her. Damn if she didn't steal his breath, as usual. Today she wore a pretty pink sundress, sparkling jewelry, and ballet slippers. A thick, dark blonde braid hung over one shoulder, and a robo-bird perched on the other.

"Have you been thinking about genitals this whole time?" he teased.

"No!" she bellowed, and he fought a grin. "I mean, I was, but only for the purposes of torture."

"Then I'm doing something wrong." Though he'd never been in a serious relationship—pretend or otherwise—he liked having a live-in girlfriend. Especially *this* girlfriend. Her mix of naïveté and street smarts charmed him, and her very presence drove him to the brink of sexual madness.

Patience. Be what she needs, and be rewarded.

Her gaze slid down his torso before lingering on the obvious erection behind his fly. She began to pant—with excitement.

They'd been courting for three days. That she'd stopped jumping away from him when he displayed sexual desire… sweet progress!

"Like what you see?" he asked.

"Yes," she whispered, the rosy blush in her cheeks deepening. "I, uh, baked you something. My first gift to you." She whispered something to the robo-bird, and the mechanical marvel flew off…only to return a few minutes later with a silver fork. "I asked Fox about your favorite dessert, and she said you love humble pie. I'd never heard of it, but thankfully Olivia found a recipe."

That damned Fox. "Olivia—Aeron's woman? I thought you weren't interested in reaching out to the Lords and Ladies."

"Olivia reached out to me. As a former SO Messenger, she can speak into people's minds, even from a great distance. Anyway. I'd never heard of a few ingredients, either, but Fox found them for me. Minced haggis, cricket flour, and lutefisk."

That was what Leila made him? For the second time since meeting her, his palate wept.

"This was my first attempt at baking, but I'm pretty sure I nailed it," she continued merrily, offering the pie and the fork. "Go ahead. Take a bite. Tell me your opinion."

Hide your grimace now. Kill Fox and Olivia later. He accepted the fork, pressed the tines into the dish, and took a tentative bite of what looked like literal shit.

Do not gag. He chewed the foul offering, then forced himself to swallow. What he wouldn't give to return to the good ol' days, and chilidogs.

"Well?" she asked.

Galen had no problem lying to people. Actually, he *preferred* to lie. The less anyone knew about him, the better. But here, now, he refused to disrespect Leila with an untruth. So, he kept eating. As long as his mouth was full, he didn't have to speak.

When he finished, she smiled. A brilliant, radiant smile.

Nausea—worth it!

"Thank you," he told her, but the nausea worsened, his stomach churning hard enough to make butter. Sweat beaded on his brow, and his upper lip. "Hey, quick question. Was arsenic included in the list of ingredients?"

Her smile vanished, and she paled. "No. Was it supposed to be?"

"Excuse me for a moment." He sprinted to his private bathroom, and vomited in the toilet.

Leila followed, sniffling and saying, "I'm so sorry."

In a haze of vomiting and pain, he lacked the wherewithal to comfort her.

"Let me help you," she pleaded, cleaning him up with a cool, damp rag. "I'll never bake again, I swear. You're going to get better. You have to get better."

His final thought before he drifted to sleep—*If this is what happens when I'm sick, I'll be requesting another humble pie just as soon as I grow a new stomach.*

* * * *

By morning, Galen had healed. He should have rejoiced. Instead, he pouted—in a super manly way. At some point during the night, Leila had muttered, "I'm going to make up for this." Then she'd left him alone in the bathroom.

Now, he scrubbed his mouth a couple dozen times, showered, and dressed.

Ready to hunt her down, he emerged—and drew up short. Leila must have worked all night. She'd filled the entire chamber with gifts. A framed collage of selfies, dueling pistols, a sword with a bejeweled hilt, and an X-rated snow globe. Best of all, she'd created a defense plan, complete with measures and counter-measures in case of a demon invasion.

My smart, vicious beauty.

He smiled. The traps she suggested were truly diabolical. Dimensions for genital traps she'd wanted him to paint. Salt and sugar mines to melt the flesh from a demon's bones. How to create invisible doorways that led to a Candyland-esque type realm, where magic made torturing others impossible.

Damn if he didn't want her at his side for every battle and war. Their enemies wouldn't stand a chance. But most of all, he wanted her in his bed. His craving for her continued to grow, consuming him bit by bit.

Galen had to up his game.

And he did.

For the rest of their test drive month, he knocked on her door at least three times a day, a new gift in hand. The skulls of the demons he'd slain in her honor. Unique pieces of jewelry he'd acquired throughout the centuries. Romance novels featuring villainous heroes who saved the day and won the girl. A bouquet of different fried meats on sticks.

Under his care, she bloomed. By the end of the month, she brightened any time he entered a room. When he touched her, she practically purred. She smiled more than she frowned.

The same changes happened to Galen. Leila quieted his demons, seeming to know every time the two acted up. As False Hope spewed poison, she spoke truth. As Jealousy darkened his mood, she shined a light in his heart with a simple smile.

This morning, Galen had a new gift for her—an offer she (hopefully) couldn't refuse. As he stood at the closed door adjoining their room, a tide of foreboding washed over him. Something very, very bad was about to happen.

Had someone invaded the realm?

Fury boiled Galen's blood as he weaponed up. Daggers. Rings with spikes. Wrist cuffs with garrote wire.

He texted Fox. **I'm scouting for invaders. Remain on alert.**

He considered texting Leila, too, then discarded the idea, opting not to frighten her with the possibility of invasion.

Determined to eliminate any threat, he strode onto his rail-less balcony. A cool, crisp breeze scented with salt, sandalwood, and honeysuckle wafted around him. Familiar. Nothing foreign. Waves crashed in the distance, and birds called. But he hesitated. Leave Leila, even for an hour or two? His chest clenched. *A warrior does what he must to protect his treasures.*

Galen dove from the ledge and flared his wings. Wind lifted him up, up, combing his hair and ruffling his feathers. He loved the freedom he found in the skies. Loved the feeling of both freefalling and soaring.

Thankfully, he found no signs of invasion. None of his traps had been triggered. Sinkholes, trip wires, and landmines.

Perhaps he should take Leila for a tour? The entire realm consisted of a pink sand beach shrouded by thick white mist, a glittering ocean of violet, and a forest of lavender wisteria trees. Two suns dotted the horizon, their amber light muted, as if twilight forever descended.

The first time Galen had come here, he'd thought, *Legion will love this.* So of course he'd killed the owner and taken possession. Might equaled right. His first order of business had been picking Leila's bedroom and filling it with all of her favorite, frilly things.

False Hope whispered, *All is well…nothing to worry about…*

Galen tensed, his sense of foreboding reaching new heights. Maybe that was the demon's true hope. To fill him with fear—a malignant cancer—and ruin his time with Leila. Over nothing!

He had a choice. Let the demon win, or make Leila laugh again. Ensure his woman was relaxed and happy, or tense and dismayed.

The fortress came into view, a massive structure with ancient stone walls. Along the copper roof, gargoyles stood sentry. Galen closed in and slowed, then angled his body to ease onto his balcony. On his feet once again, he snapped his wings into his sides.

After stowing the weapons, he returned to the door that joined his bedroom to Leila's. His ear twitched, picking up the light pitter-patter of footsteps. Finally, only a whisper of air separated them. Today, she wore a plain white T-shirt and nothing else.

For a moment, his thoughts derailed. *Look at those bronzed, mile-long legs, ready to wrap around my waist. Or my shoulders.*

"Are you hungry? You must be hungry," he said. He wanted to watch her eat again. And yeah, okay, staring at someone as they savored a meal was probably creep-city, but Leila was his addiction, the sickness in his blood, and there was no cure. Symptoms included:

Acute swelling in the groin—Check.

Night and day sweats—Check.

Total lack of concentration—Check.

"I'm not hungry," she said, and sniffled.

Sniffled? He forced his gaze back up her body, only to curse. Red rimmed her eyes, and tears glistened on her cheeks. *Clench.* He cupped her jaw and demanded, "What's wrong?"

"Everything! You've been so good to me, but now our test drive month is over. You probably want to sleep with me just so you can be done with me and and and—"

Not knowing what else to do, he pressed a swift kiss to her lips. She gasped, the pulse at the base of her throat hammering.

Could the month's end be the reason for his foreboding? "Do you want to know my favorite day in all the eons of my life? The day you doctored me. And the day after that, when you smiled at me. And the day after that, just because you were at my side. I wouldn't change anything that's happened between us—except asking for more than a month of your time."

Her eyes widened. "Really?"

Nod. "How about we extend the test drive another month?"

"Yes. Absolutely." She leaned against him, resting her cheek against his pec. An intimate pose, one she'd instigated. "You are becoming my favorite part of every day, too."

The rightness of her words...the fit of her body against his... He nearly howled with triumph. *Steady*. Moving slowly, languidly, as if he hadn't a care, he wrapped his arms around her. She offered no protests, and didn't tense, so he took things a step further and ran his fingers through her silken curls.

Sighing, she cuddled closer.

The scent of wildflowers ignited little fires inside him. "Get changed and meet me in the gym," he said, kissing her temple. "I'm going to give you a self-defense lesson." *And put my hands all over your delectable body.*

"That would be amazing." With a squeal of happiness, she leaped up to kiss his cheek. Then she backtracked and shut the door in his face, leaving him shocked to his core.

How easily she'd just touched him. How easily she'd offered affection. So different from the frightened girl he'd found in that cabin.

Whistling under his breath, he strode to the gym. Along the way, he spotted the things Leila had left lying around. A piece of her jewelry here, one of her shoes there. A sequined top draped over the couch. A ruffled skirt atop a chair. The sight did something strange to his blackened heart.

The organ came back to life.

In a very short amount of time, Leila had become a necessary part of his family. Though she and Fox didn't always get along, they tolerated each other so...win.

He removed his tunic—*better to tempt you with, my dear*—as well as the razor blades in his wings. No way he would risk cutting her. Needing a distraction while he waited, he whaled on the punching bag, working up a good sweat. Maybe, if he expelled enough energy, he wouldn't get a hard-on every time he touched her.

Nah. He had to face facts. With a female like Leila, he would be sporting wood for all eternity.

Half an hour later, she strolled into the gym. She'd pulled her mass of hair into a ponytail and donned a pink tank and a teeny-tiny pair of shorts, those mile-long legs still on magnificent display. And yeah, he got a hard-on.

"Ready for your lesson?" he asking, his blood singing with anticipation.

"Muscles," she blurted out, then gasped. A lovely shade of rose spilled over her cheeks, brighter than ever before. "I mean, yes. Please."

More and more, she'd begun to see him as a sexual being. Which was only fair. Galen obsessed about every inch of her.

He rubbed a hand over the two butterfly tattoos etched into his chest, their wings riding the ridges of his muscles. The mark of his demons. Her gaze followed the action, and he fought a grin.

Of course, False Hope seized the opportunity to build him up. *Teach her how to defend herself, and she will have no need of you. She'll leave the realm. She'll—*

Leila framed his face with her delicate hands and said, "Thank you for this newest gift. I will be forever grateful."

The demon quieted, and Galen huffed out a breath.

"You're welcome," he said, then frowned. "Why did you remove your baubles? It's important to train while you wear them, so you'll know what to do if someone attempts to use them against you."

"Good point. I'll wear them next time, promise." She swiped her hands together, a case-closed gesture. "Do you, uh, want to put on a shirt before we get started?"

And deny himself the ecstasy of skin-to-skin contact? Never. "I'm going to work up even more of a sweat. There's no reason to dirty a shirt. Laundry, amirite?" He stretched out his wings, wrapping the ends around her calves to urge her closer. "Besides, I would never deprive you of my beauty. Unless you're unable to control your reactions to my touch?"

"I think it's a distinct possibility," she admitted, and almost looked…entranced by his wings. She grazed her fingers over the outer edge. "So soft."

He shuddered with pleasure and urged her closer. "Do you trust me, Leila?" He continued to caress her calf, his feathers gliding up and down, urging her even closer. And, with every upward glide, he gained new ground. Finally, the tips brushed the perfect globes of her ass.

"I do. I trust you." She gripped his shoulders to steady herself. "But I also… *don't* trust you."

Smart. He might act like a tame house cat around her, but a hungry lion lurked inside him. "Tell me, Professor Sugar Tush. How I can earn an A plus in Leila's Trust 101?"

She laughed, saying, "It's Dr. McGyna to you." But she quickly sobered and nibbled on her bottom lip.

He had to bite his tongue to stop himself from replacing her teeth with his own.

"Why do you want my trust so badly?" she asked. Almost absentmindedly, she toyed with the ends of his hair.

"You know why." Blood smoldering. Wings, still gliding. Up, down. Up, down, drawing goose bumps to the surface of her skin. "Say it."

Her gaze met his. He watched, transfixed, as her pupils expanded, like a dark raincloud sweeping over a desert. The blush spread down her throat, where her pulse picked up speed. Her breaths turned shallow. "You want me in your bed."

"That's right. I want you. I want *inside* you."

She moved her hands to his pecs, as if she meant to push him away. Instead, she buried her nails in his flesh to hold him still. His Leila was a born predator. She'd simply forgotten for a while.

"All you want from me is sex?" she asked.

"All I have to *offer* is sex." And more enemies. If he made their relationship official, he would put a large target on her back, and a huge bounty on her head.

And what about a family? Did she want children one day? Galen sucked at being a parent.

Hey, kids. You'll have to excuse Dad for a sec. He's got to wash the brain matter off his hands.

"Do you think there's a possibility, even slight, that we are forever mates?" she asked.

Her tone...he heard the percolation of hope. Courtesy of the demon?

"Do you *want* to be forever mates?" Damn. He heard the percolation of hope in *his* tone as well.

"I don't know. Maybe? Aeron and Olivia are so happy together. *All* of the Lords and their mates are happy. Ecstatically so."

"I'm not like other Lords." He settled one hand on her waist and reached out with the other, letting his fingers hover over her lips. When she gave an almost imperceptible nod of encouragement, he traced a fingertip from one corner of her mouth to the other. "At heart, they are good. Perfect. I'm not."

Reminding him of the Leila he'd first met, *she* took a step closer to *him*, ensuring *nothing* separated them, not even a whisper. Her body pressed against his. As they breathed each other's air, their hearts raced in sync.

"I don't want perfect," she said, her voice low and husky. "I want *perfect for me.*"

Was he perfect for her? Were they perfect for *each other*? The man who'd once pretended to be an angel and the woman who'd once been an actual devil. Or did she belong with some nameless, faceless male who wouldn't disrupt her life?

Whoever he is, kill him, Jealousy demanded. *Rip off his limbs, so he can never touch her. Cut out his tongue, so he can never kiss her. Neuter him!*

Leila must have sensed the spike of violence. She plucked her nails free of his pecs and stepped back, severing contract.

Calm. Steady. "Still afraid of me? If I didn't hurt you after you tried to murder me with a humble pie, I'll *never* hurt you." He would offer the reminder as many times as necessary.

For a moment, amusement replaced trepidation in her eyes. But she sobered as quickly as before, and said, "I know you won't hurt me. At least, I *think* I know. Logically. But your demons…sometimes I'm not sure I can trust what you make me feel."

His heart leaped. "What do I make you feel, hmm?"

A beat of silence. "Desire," she finally admitted. "*Sexual* desire."

A thousand emotions hit him at once. At the forefront? Utter satisfaction unlike anything he'd ever known. "Give me time, sugar. I'll prove your feelings are genuine." Or he would die trying.

He would tempt and tease her until she ached without his touch. Until she craved him like a drug.

The way she once craved Aeron.

Galen curled his hands into fists. *Hate Jealousy!*

"Then," he continued, "when you want more of what I'm offering, you have only to tell me, and I'll give you more." So much more. He might give her everything. Despite the complications, despite the dangers.

The thought left him uneasy at first; it was so different than what he'd allowed himself to want, or expect. But it stretched and reclined inside his head, getting comfortable. He'd never offered "everything" to anyone. Spirit, heart, and body. Past, present, future. All that he was, all that he would be. All that he owned. Too many times his hopes and dreams had crashed and burned. If he placed those hopes and dreams in

Leila's hands, and she abandoned him, he might not ever recover.

Bottom line, she was a flight risk.

Take what you want and abandon ship. Get in, get out. At least he would leave her better off than he'd found her. Another first for him.

"Why are *you* willing to give *me* time?" she asked. "Why do you continue to want me? Why haven't I scared you off?"

"I don't understand the question. Why *wouldn't* I want you? You are smart. You taught yourself how to read and write. Yes, I know about that. You are wily. A survivor. You are beautiful, luscious, every inch of you tailor-made for me. You are ballsy."

She withered, her shoulders rolling in. "No, I *used* to be ballsy. Now I'm just a weak link."

"You were hurt in the worst possible way, your spirit broken. But you are putting the pieces back together, and that makes you my hero."

Tears welled, and her chin trembled. For the second time, she stepped closer to him. When she rested her forehead against his sternum, he enfolded her soft, sexy body in his arms.

"You are unlike anyone else I've ever known," he continued. "The perfect combination of charm, vulnerability, and hard-on inducing temper. When we're done with our lessons, you'll be able to dissuade anyone who makes you feel threatened, even me." He kissed her brow. "Do you have any experience with self-defense?"

"Tons. I grew up in hell, home to liars, thieves, murderers, and—" She winced, and he didn't have to wonder what she'd planned to say. Rapists. "If you didn't protect your stuff, you lost it."

"We'll consider this a refresher course, then. Are you ready?"

A beat of silence, then a nod.

He wasn't sure she was, but he was going to train her, anyway. "Let's say a man grabs your throat with both hands to choke you out. What do you do?"

"Do I have a blade, or am I weaponless?"

"Weaponless."

"Then I twist off his nuts and run."

Ouch. "What if you can't reach his testicles?"

"I jab my fingers into his eye sockets, rip out his eyeballs, and run."

All right. Her past experience featured a lot of groin play and running. Noted. "Let's start with a forward-facing grab. I'm going to place my hands at your throat. All right?"

Though pale, she acquiesced once again. So he did as promised, settling his fingers on the vulnerable column of her neck. Gentle, so gentle. Immediately her pulse jumped, and her breathing changed. He despised the flash of fear in her eyes.

"First, you must subdue your panic." For a long while, he remained as still as a statue, letting her grow accustomed to the heat of his skin and the weight of his touch.

Only when the tension faded from her expression did he trace his thumbs around and around her pulse. "Good. Now, move one leg back and drop your body weight as much as possible while bending your knees." When she'd complied, he said, "Bring one arm over my arms and rotate."

"Like this?" She executed a perfect rotation, forcing him to loosen his grip.

"Just like that." Excellent. "Next you'll use the same arm to elbow me anywhere you can reach. Don't worry about aim. Just throw your elbow as many times as necessary until you are freed."

When she executed the move flawlessly, Galen breathed a sigh of relief. She *had* learned dirty street fighting in hell, the skills had just been buried underneath a mountain of fear. Today, the mountain came down.

For hours, they worked on hand-to-hand combat, and varied the weapons they utilized, everything from daggers to semi-automatics. He showed her every underhanded trick he knew while purposely maneuvering her into compromising positions, drawing her fears to the surface, one after the other.

Whenever she whimpered, he felt as if his guts had been ripped out. Still he pressed on. And so did she. Results had never been so critical. *Cruel to be kind.*

The first time he took her to the floor, she froze, petrified. The second time, she erupted in a panic, and she swung a fist blindly, nailing him in the eye, nearly breaking his nose.

"I'm so sorry," she said between panting breaths.

"No worries."

"Enough. Let's rest. I need a break."

"Not yet." Giving up now would only add fuel to the fire of her fear.

"I'm tired."

"So?"

"So we've played enough for one day."

"Played?" he echoed, voice hollow. They were fighting for her life.

For *their* lives.

"Yes. Played. Humans say winning or losing isn't important, only how you play the game. Well, I'm playing badly, and I want a chance to recharge."

"That is a ridiculous idiotism."

"Do you mean *idiom*?"

"No, I mean idiotism. You are to play to win, always, without exception. You give the game your all, and you never ever back down. An opponent will never let you take a time out."

She inhaled sharply, exhaled heavily, and nodded. "All right. We will continue."

He gently chucked her under the chin, almost bursting with pride. Look how far she'd come. "Give me your best, not just what's good enough. And never hesitate to use your venomous bite. You might be punched, but the perpetrator won't be able to remain on his feet for long."

The third time he took her to the floor, she was just as terrified as before. But he kept going, kept taking her down, and soon anger took hold—anger directed at them both.

"I'm going to pulverize your liver," she bellowed, shaking a fist in his direction.

He masked a grin. "Please. Try."

By the twenty-fourth time, she was fighting back, purposely swinging at him whenever she landed. If she failed to make contact, she tried to bite him, just as he'd instructed. The little vixen would have succeeded, too, had Galen not secured her hands over her head, limiting her range of motion.

He knew the exact moment she realized his muscular weight pinned her to the floor and every move she made caused their bodies to rub together, nearly driving him mad with pleasure. She stilled, little gasping breaths escaping her. Spurred by fear?

"Want me to get off?" he asked, and he wasn't sure which meaning he ascribed to the question. *Cruel to be kind, remember?* Though he disgusted himself, he pasted a leer on his face. "*Make* me get off. Unless you're too weak? Yeah, I bet that's it. You're at my mercy. Mercy I've never had." *Shut up! Enough! You're pushing too hard.*

So incredibly hard.

"I can do anything I want to you," he taunted, "and there's nothing you can do to stop me."

Those panting breaths quickened. "Galen," she croaked, nearly breaking his heart. "I want... I need..." She arched her back, purposely rubbing against him.

A broken moan left her parted lips, shocking the hell out of him. She wasn't the tiniest bit afraid. *Desire* ruled her.

Groaning, he circled his hips to grind his erection between her legs. The pleasure...the pain. *I'm dying. No, I'm dying* happy.

"You can stop me," he said. "Leila, stop me! Prove you can. Then you can do whatever you want to me. Whatever you need."

What happened next happened in a blink. Without broadcasting her intent, Leila slammed her forehead into his chin. Stars winked through his line of sight and blood filled his mouth. She worked one of her legs between their bodies, drawing her knee up, up. Then she kicked him in the face, rattling his brain against his skull. He stopped seeing stars, a black abyss threatening to swallow him whole.

The next thing he knew, *Leila* had pinned *him*. He lay flat on his back, panting, his burst of pain fading. He peered up at her, pride overwhelming him. "You did it," he said, and smiled. "You protected yourself."

Her gaze remained glued to his lips. Voice filled with smoke and gravel, she said, "I want..."

"Tell me, Leila." *Please*. "What do you want?"

Now her gaze flipped up to his, revealing endless pools of heat and hope. "I want *more*."

Chapter Eight

The moment Galen's wing had first caressed Legion's skin, pressure had begun building inside her. Who was she kidding? Pressure had been building since the moment he'd rescued her. No, *before* he'd rescued her. Since the moment they'd met.

Today, pressure had roused heat. Heat had roused tingles, a racing heart, and a never-ending ache between her legs.

Now, Galen flipped her over, pinning her down just as before. His wings blocked out the rest of the world. Any hint of her distanced and controlled self-defense teacher—gone. In his place, a ruthless seducer.

"Are you sure you want this? Are you sure you want *me*?" With one hand, he held himself steady. With the other, he cupped her breast and teased her throbbing nipple with his thumb.

"I am." Desire chased away any lingering fear. This man... oh, this man. He was the epitome of carnality, lines of tension branching from his eyes and the erotic slash of his mouth. His pale hair was messy, his cerulean eyes bright. Sweat glistened on his skin.

What made him most beautiful, however? He was as vulnerable to her as she was to him.

With his words, his actions, he'd empowered her and set her ablaze. In hell, she'd been an object. To Galen, she was a treasure.

I can forge a life with him. A good one. We can be happy.

She cried out with want. Yes, yes. A good life. Happiness. Old desires reignited, the very reasons she'd risked everything to acquire this human body. She could have a family of her own. If she worked hard enough, she could be queen of her castle, so strong no one could ever make her do anything she didn't want to do.

Of course, Galen could lose interest in her at any time. Her heart tripped over her ribs. No Galen, no family. He could choose to be with another woman, leaving the queen without her king.

Instant recognition—Jealousy at work.

Focusing on the exquisite pleasure that seethed inside her, she reiterated her demand. "I want more. Now! Give it to me."

"Yes." He swooped down, and pressed his lips against hers. Their tongues dueled, the sweetness of his taste unraveling any lingering reservations.

Her puckered nipples grazed his chest when she inhaled. Since she was panting, she inhaled *a lot*. Every breath proved shallower than the last. A scorching current electrified her cells. Her limbs quivered. Inside her, the pressure and heat only escalated.

She wound her arms around him, clinging to the only man who'd ever wanted her. The *real* her. The only man who'd ever known the real her. Who'd made her come alive with a simple touch.

"Even better than before," he rasped against her lips.

Yes, yes. But then, she knew him as a person now, not as an enemy.

He…it…*this* felt so good, no, great, no, incredible; she couldn't think beyond the moment. He was hard as a rock. He smelled like paradise. And his hands—those big, callused hands. One tangled in her hair, the other moved to her waist. Both held her tightly, reverently, as if he'd never handled such a valuable prize. So different from—

No! *Do not let the past intrude on the present.*

"Leila." His black magic voice pulled her under his spell. "Can't get enough of you."

Her body cradled his. Bowing her back, she spread her trembling legs. He ground his erection against the epicenter of her world, sending more tingling heat careening through her. Heaven on earth.

"You like this," he said, and she wasn't sure if he meant the words as a statement or a question. "You like me."

For a "selfish bastard"—Aeron's favorite Galenism, not hers—Galen sure did give more than he took. Then her thoughts fragmented, her mind only processing one word at a time. Sublime. Glorious. Blissful. "Galen." Somehow, his name perfectly encapsulated each of the descriptors.

"Yes, Leila." He nipped the line of her jaw, then ran the lobe of her ear between his teeth. "Always yes."

As she purred her approval, he returned his attention to her lips. Desperation tinged their next kiss. With more and more aggression, he rolled his tongue against hers. So good! The bliss…

Gyrating against his length faster and faster, she threaded her fingers through his silken hair, scraped her nails along his back and over the downy-soft feathers in his snow-white wings. He stilled, his eyes closed, an expression of absolute rapture overtaking his face. So she did it again. Gyrate. Glide. Scrape.

He shuddered and lifted his head, blond locks tumbling over his forehead. When she reached up to smooth away the errant strands, he nuzzled her palm. A gesture of affection, not just lust.

So this is what ecstasy feels like.

A moment later, he was kissing her again, flooding her with more bliss, drowning her in more ecstasy. He kneaded her breasts, the warmth of his skin seeping through her tank. The blood in her veins turned molten, and her bones liquified.

"Let's get you more comfortable." He ripped off her top, then her bra.

Cool air caressed her fevered flesh. Yes! Dual sensations. Too much, not enough.

Looking her over, he made an animalistic sound. "Made for me." He traced a finger around one nipple, then moved to the other, and her entire body jerked. Where his hands touched, his mouth followed.

He laved; he bit lightly. All the while, she writhed beneath him, chasing an orgasm.

"No female compares to you." He leaned to the side just enough to glide that naughty finger around her navel, again and again. Desire soaked her feminine core. Aches consumed her.

"Galen." His name was both a plea and a curse. Legion knew she should reciprocate, maybe flick her fingers over his nipples, maybe reach between their bodies and grip his massive erection, but her nails were currently embedded in his broad shoulders, and she loved having them there. Predatory instinct demanded she hold her male in place until he'd satisfied her.

"When I finally get inside you," he said, his breaths as labored as hers, "you won't have to bite me to kill me. Pleasure will do the job."

"Yes. Inside me," she pleaded.

"I'm not going to take you, not today. I'm going to prove I can maintain strict control with you, no matter the cost to my sanity. I'm going to make you come. Do you trust me enough to see to your pleasure in other ways?"

She pried apart her eyelids to probe his features. The strain in his beautiful face had sharpened, and a storm brewed in those sky blue irises. His lips were red and slightly swollen from their kisses.

He's mine, and I left my mark. "I-I trust you enough," she finally replied.

Groaning, he ripped open the fly of his leathers and slipped his long, iron hard length beneath her shorts and panties. Hardness met softness, heat met heat. Maddened by desire, she hissed in a breath.

"Ah, sugar, you are drenched." He rewarded her with a wicked smile. The kind of wicked a fallen angel might use to tempt another angel into falling. The kind of wicked she hadn't known she'd craved until now. "If I do something you don't like, tell me and I'll stop."

Nails, sinking deeper. "Just…hurry!"

He didn't remove her remaining garments, just rolled his hips so that the head of his shaft pressed against her aching core, once, twice. Lances of excruciating pleasure shot through her, creating a fervor of anticipation.

When would he make her come?

He withdrew his length from her panties, wrenching a groan from her chest.

No, no, no! "Galen!"

"I'm not done with you, sugar." He sank a finger deep, deep inside her.

"Yes!"

In, out. He spread her moisture over her clitoris. In, out. With the next inward glide, he plunged in a second finger, and she cried out. The two digits stretched her. In, out. In, out.

"The things you make me crave," he said between panting breaths. As he wedged in a third finger, he pressed his thumb against the heart of her need. "I'm helpless against your allure."

Just. Like. That. The ache and pressure collided, a bomb of ecstasy exploding inside her. She shook, lost in the throes of passion. Muscles clenched and unclenched on bone. White-hot heat enveloped her. Her inner walls tightened around his fingers, as if unwilling to part with him.

Nothing had ever felt this good, her body a live wire of sensation. She soared to the stars, until she crashed and shattered. Her defenses— gone.

Since her rescue from hell, emotions had plagued her. Hate, rage and helplessness. A corrosive brew, always festering. Here, now, with her barriers disintegrated, all three surged through her, leaving her raw and agonized.

Galen withdrew his fingers to spread her essence over her bottom lip. To her astonishment—and delight—he licked where he'd touched. A deliciously scandalous act. One that grounded her in the moment, and the frenzy of need, letting the past recede.

"Hit me," he commanded softly. "You need to purge, and I need to feel your fury. When you needed me most, I failed to save you."

Now the past came rushing back, joining the emotional deluge. "I sh-should have saved *myself*."

"Sometimes we *can't* save ourselves. I've been locked in multiple dungeons, bound by chains. Once, a dragon shifter burned me alive every time I regenerated. I've been staked to a table, my torso cut open from sternum to pubic bone, so that demons could feast on my organs."

She cringed. "In hell, that particular torture is known as the All You Can Eat Buffet Experience."

"And that isn't the worst of it. I've had all of my teeth extracted with pliers, and my genitals removed with gardening shears. To this day, a certain Greek goddess uses my sac as a coin purse."

Now Legion barked out a laugh, only to jolt from shock. "How can you turn a terrible moment into a joyous one?"

"It's a gift." He kissed her temple, a gesture he'd made before. This time, he followed up the action with a kiss on the tip of her nose, then her chin, as if staking a claim on each individual feature. *This time*, her heart ached. "My point is, sometimes a self-save isn't possible for a thousand different reasons, but none of those reasons mean you are lacking. Our heart, mind, and body can only take so much. And that's okay. It happens to us all. That is why family and friends are so important. They help us when we need it most. Then, when they need help, we return the favor."

Her eyes misted over, and stomach fluttered. Blood suddenly hot and cold. His every word a caress, but also a searing poker to her inner wounds. The juxtaposition left her dazed.

"Hit me," he repeated.

"Never!"

"Hit me! For centuries, I've been an instigator of pain. Now I'd rather bear the brunt of yours."

"No," she said, but even as the denial echoed between them, she swung. Her fist rammed into his shoulder. Before her mind had time to process the crashing wave of horror—I *just punched the man who pleasured me*—her other hand was swinging toward his face.

With a sob, Legion unleashed, hitting and hitting and hitting.

"That's my girl." Blood wet his teeth.

Hitting, harder and harder. She'd never shared her heartbreak with another. She'd never *wanted* to share, had only ever wanted to forget. As she shared the pain with Galen, festering inner wounds hurt a little less.

His eye swelled, and blood blurred his vision. A knot formed in his jaw. "Let the hurt out. Every bit of it."

Hitting, harder still, until the last of her strength drained, and she sagged against the floor. Voice ragged, she whispered, "I'm sorry, I'm so sorry."

He scooped her into his arms, stood, and carried her to the living room, where he eased onto a chair designed to accommodate his wings. For a long while, he simply held her. Neither of them spoke.

"I'm sorry," she said with more force. "No matter what you believe, you didn't deserve my wrath."

"And you didn't deserve the terrible things Lucifer and his demons did to you." Again, he kissed the tip of her nose, her cheek, the corner of her mouth.

See! Staking a claim. These feather-light brushes of his lips beamed bright lights of anticipation into her withered heart, revealing a truth she'd forgotten. Life didn't have to be an endless parade of bad moments. After a storm, flowers bloomed.

Maybe False Hope was responsible for the shift in her mood, maybe not. Probably not. There was no hint of the fiend's usual fear.

"I want to tell you what happened to me." The tears spilled over, scalding her cheeks.

He tensed. "This is going to destroy me, but that's okay. We'll put each other back together."

Back together. Yes. She wanted that. So she did it. She told him. How she was blindfolded and often staked to an altar. The way demons had laughed and taunted her. The way they had poked and prodded at her…the many ways they had violated her. How she'd never known what fresh hell would be visited upon her, the wait sometimes even more agonizing than the actual torture.

At first, she'd prayed for Aeron to save her. After a while, she'd hoped Galen would do the honors, despite the terrible way things had ended between them. *Then* she'd prayed for a quick death. But death had never come knocking, her tormentors careful to ensure her human body survived each new horror. Eventually, she'd resigned herself to a pain-filled eternity.

Galen listened, his muscles knotting. Her teeth began to chatter, even though she wasn't cold, and he tightened his grip.

"I'm sorry I wasn't there for you." Gentle, so gentle, he wiped away her tears. "Their actions speak of their evil, not yours. Your worth was not tarnished by what they did."

He sounded certain. 100%, zero doubts in his mind. Legion wasn't convinced. "As a demon, I tortured countless souls. Later, I tried to murder you. Maybe I *did* deserve what was—"

"No. You didn't. But let's say you're right. Let's say you deserved everything that happened and more. Why did those particular demons deserve to mete out your punishment? What gave them the right to judge you for your crimes?"

Good question. "Nothing?"

"That's right. Nothing." The minty freshness of his breath caressed the crown of her head. "You love the Lords despite the crimes they committed in the past, yet you judge yourself so harshly."

Wow, did this brute have a confounding number of layers. And, by some miracle, she began to believe he was… right. No one had the right to cast stones at her. No one had the right to violate her body.

The realization caused the floodgates to open anew, and she sobbed all over again. He petted her hair, stroked her back, and enfolded her with wings, the feathers caressing one side of her body while his intoxicating scent filled her nose.

By the time her tears dried, her eyes were puffy, her nose stuffy. Exhausted and sniffling, she sagged against him. "Galen?"

"Yes, Leila?"

She paused to double check her desires. Did she really want to suggest what she was about to suggest? Yes! "I think we should end the test part of our relationship and try for real."

* * * *

"I agree." The words rushed from his mouth, an unstoppable freight train. As he held this beautiful woman in his arms, rocking her back and forth, she moved to the #1 spot on his list of treasures.

She's mine. I keep what's mine.

"Out with the temporary arrangement," he said, "and in with the permanent commitment."

He wanted this woman. Physically. Emotionally. Mentally.

Eternally.

Ending their association had never been an option for him; he just hadn't wanted to admit it before, had feared being rejected. But to let her go, he would have to rip out the best part of his heart and soul, becoming half a man.

Hell, Leila wasn't just #1 on his list. She was everything to him, her needs and desires more important to him than his own. He didn't care if it was healthy or not. He cared about *her*. Galen would do whatever proved necessary to protect her from the ramifications of an association with him.

When she'd come apart in his arms, gasping his name and clinging to his body, her tight inner walls clamping on his fingers, something inside him had changed. Contentment had beckoned, closer than ever before.

Fox was right. Leila was magic.

Every day since she'd moved in, he'd woken up brimming with anticipation, wondering what she would say or do next. The stunning beauty had turned mundane tasks into mini-adventures and meals into living fantasies. Each night, when he'd placed his head on a pillow, he'd fallen asleep with a smile, replaying their interactions.

Galen might have been created for war, but he lived for Leila. His everything, he thought again. She meant more to him than any war, title, or kingdom. Because...

Yeah. Every part of him loved every part of her. No one had ever fit him so perfectly. She had become his greatest strength, and his favorite weakness. A true beacon of hope.

The knowledge kicked him into a tailspin of excitement rather than panic. His future had never looked so bright. She soothed the ravages of his soul, and satisfied the man who'd always wanted more.

So they'd had a rough start. So what? The end mattered more than the beginning.

Not that they would end. She had trusted him with her passion; now he would fight for her heart.

You'll never make a relationship work. Soon she'll remember you are a betrayer. Galen the Treacherous. She'll leave.

"You tensed," Leila said, tracing her fingertips along the stubble on his jaw. "Are you all right?"

He buried his face in the hollow of her neck, clinging to the woman who owned his future. "When you are with me? Yes."

* * * *

Awash with vulnerability, Legion traced her fingertips along the shell of Galen's ear. "When we kissed, I climaxed, but you didn't."

"Believe me, I am keenly aware of this," he replied, his tone dry.

"Well...I want to make you come."

He winked at her, desire ablaze in his irises. "Yes. I want you to. Need you to." But he frowned. "Do you hear that?"

He didn't give her a chance to respond, just jumped to his feet, grabbed her shirt and yanked it over her head before pushing her behind him and zipping his pants. As he palmed two daggers, footsteps registered. So many, blending together, moving at a clipped pace.

Fear chilled her to the bone. An invasion?

"Run," he commanded, flaring his wings. "Hide. Now!"

Part of her shouted, *Yes! Run! Now, now, now.* The other part of her simmered with a fierce tide of rage. How dare anyone interrupt the most beautiful moment of her life?

She wouldn't leave Galen to fight the coming battle on his own. And there would be a battle. Aggression charged the air.

Though she trembled, she planted her feet, determined. *I will stand. I will fight for this man.* No matter the cost.

Glass shattered. An entire wall crumbled, and over a hundred men stormed into the living room. One man occupied the center of the group. He had dark hair, bronzed skin, and a cold, calculated smile. Cronus, the former king of the Titans. Or rather, his clone. How had he opened a portal to get here?

More powerful than we realized...

"So nice to see you again, Galen." The Titan's smile grew colder. "I knew putting a contract on your life you would lead me to my prize." With a snap of his fingers, the army launched forward—advancing on *Legion.*

Chapter Nine

What is happening?

Legion stood as motionless as a statue, her good intentions pulverized. Fear overshadowed rage.

Galen had no such difficulties. He acted fast, bending down to clasp the hilt of a sword that had been anchored to the underside of the coffee table.

How many weapons were hidden in this place, and where could *she* get one?

Like you could do any damage. Helpless...

Galen fought the soldiers with masterful skill. But then, he had the heart of a warrior, and the soul of a predator. The limbs of their enemies thudded to the floor. Blood flowed. Bellows of pain and agony created a horrifying chorus.

And still she remained in place, her heartbeat warped, her stomach in knots.

More soldiers swarmed Galen. So many. Too many. Swords arced toward him, one after the other. He ducked and parried, all while shielding her. No matter how many injuries he sustained, he kept fighting.

Why did Cronus want her? Why go to so much trouble?

Was she going to do nothing for the man who'd just pleasured and comforted her? Who'd encouraged and praised her. Or would she find a way to push through her terror and save him?

Metal whistled through the air—*slice*. Galen roared, his wrist detaching from his arm. A second later, his hand plopped to the rug with a sickening thud.

Legion screamed, horror shredding what remained of her calm.

"St-stop," she cried. "Please! I'll…I'll go with you. Just leave Galen alone."

"No," her winged warrior shouted.

The same cry echoed inside her head. Still she peered at Cronus and pleaded, "Don't hurt him any more."

Though blood spurted from a severed artery, weakening him, Galen continued fighting until his knees gave out, and he dropped.

Close to vomiting, Legion leaped in front of him and spread her arms. Breathing was nearly impossible now, the air too thick. Her lungs shuddered, burned, and seized, rejecting what little oxygen she'd managed to draw in.

In a blink, Cronus appeared at her side. He pinched her chin to turn her face one way, then the other.

Still on his knees, Galen tried to stab the king's midsection. But his reflexes had slowed dramatically, and his aim was off. Probably dizzy. Cronus easily deflected both blows.

"I said stop! If you kill Galen," she croaked, "I will fight you. Whatever you want from me, I'll do everything in my power to ensure you never get it."

She had to get the Titan and his men out of here, so Galen could summon Fox.

A shrug of the king's wide shoulders. No man had ever been so smug. "Fight me or not. Makes no difference to me. Either way, I will get what I want."

"Are you sure?" *Think, think.* How to get him out? "Wh-what is it you want, exactly?"

"I want many things from you, she-demon, for you are a rare and wonderful creature. The best of humans, the best of immortals."

"I don't understand." Could she drag and toss Galen out the window, giving *him* a chance to run? She'd have to do it fast enough that none of the soldiers could take a swing at him.

Galen struggled to rise, still refusing to give up. A soldier kicked him in the face. Breath heaved from him in a single gust, and blood sprayed from his mouth. Legion swallowed a cry of distress.

"Think of it. I can scrap you for parts," Cronus said casually, as if a man wasn't bleeding to death at his feet. "If I remove your teeth, I can adhere venomous enamel to different weapons. I can extract your marrow, and create my own army of demons. A legion commanded by me, and me alone. I can use your bones as shivs. For what can slay a demon? Another demon. The possibilities are endless."

Her chest tightened, the urge to vomit bombarding her. "You wouldn't go to this much trouble for such things."

And still Galen struggled to rise.

"You are right." Cronus kneed the underside of Galen's chin, sending him back to the floor. "I want inside your head. You have secrets I *will* unearth."

She tried to dive on her man, but one of the soldiers grabbed her arm to lock her in place. Galen wheezed as he met her gaze, and it was clear speech was no longer possible for him. Words weren't needed, however. In his eyes, she saw grief, remorse, and fury; he would rather die fighting than watch as the Titan used her for anything.

"If you walk away now, without killing him, or hurting him further," she rasped, "I won't wipe my memory." A bluff, and a downright dirty lie. Maybe it would work, maybe it wouldn't. But she had to try. The only way to sell your lies? Confidence. "You know Cameo, former keeper of Misery? The demon wiped her mind anytime she experienced happiness. That is a demon trick. I retained my demon qualities, remember? I can erase everything *at will*. There'll be nothing left to unearth." What secrets did he want? She had none.

Cronus stared at her, hard, a muscle jumping in his jaw. "Very well," he finally said. Then he vanished and reappeared, flashing directly behind Galen to slam a dagger hilt into his temple.

Her beautiful warrior slumped over, his eyes closing. He would have crash-landed if she hadn't wrenched free of the solider and caught him, easing him down.

Hot tears burned her cheeks. She ripped material from the hem of her shirt, planning to bind his forearm. Blood continued to spurt from his severed artery. But strong arms snaked around her, dragging her backward.

The last glimpse she had of Galen, he lay on the floor, face down, blood pooling around him.

* * * *

Galen blinked open his eyes. A milky film clouded his vision while searing pain circulated through his entire body. Groaning, he reached up to wipe his face—

One of his hands was missing.

Memories thundered inside his head, and he jerked. Leila's wonder as she orgasmed. Her fury as she'd whaled on him. Her pain as she'd shared her past. Cronus's invasion. The army.

Shock twined with terror, ice spreading through his cells. Men had swarmed him, and though he'd fought, fought with every ounce of strength he possessed, Galen had failed to save Leila.

You've got this, False Hope had said. And he'd believed the fiend, because he'd known he would do anything, cross any line, to ensure his woman's safety. Now...

Her past could be repeating itself, and I can do nothing to stop it. He threw back his head and roared at the ceiling.

Her dread had been palpable, yet it hadn't prevented her from bargaining with Cronus. Just to save Galen's life. He'd let her down, but still she'd fought for him.

What secrets did the former king hope to uncover?

And scrap her for parts? Galen would die first!

A strip of material rested on the floor. A piece of Leila's shirt. She must have tried to bind his wound. He wrapped his wrist, using his teeth to tie the ends together, then labored to his feet. Torrents of dizziness nearly knocked him down. The broken bones in both legs didn't help.

He'd lost a hand before. Actually, he'd lost entire limbs before. In a few weeks, the appendage would regrow. But there was no way he would wait to go after Leila. If Fox helped him gear up, then opened a portal, he could recruit the Lords within minutes. They would aid him, no questions asked. Not for him, but for Leila.

You can't save her. You are too weak. Regain your strength before you challenge a Titan.

Hate False Hope! The fiend longed to hobble him with fear. Galen wouldn't rest until Leila was safe. To start, he needed his cell phone.

He stumbled down the hall, heading for his bedroom, leaving a trail of blood behind him. On the stairs, his knees weakened, and he nearly collapsed. Just a little farther...

Finally. Success. He fired off a one-handed text to Fox, gathered his emergency kit, and plopped onto the foot of the bed, where he once again used his teeth to tighten a tourniquet around his forearm.

A portal opened, a curtain of air peeling back. Fox stepped into the bedroom, took one look at him, and cursed. "What happened?" Behind her, the portal snapped closed, a hard gust of wind sweeping through the room.

"Cronus 2.0 found us. Must have a Gatekeeper on his staff, or he uses more magic than we realized. He took Leila—Legion. Now I need to get to Aeron."

Moving at the speed of light, Fox started a fire in the hearth, heated a dagger, then cauterized his raw, open wound. While he bellowed curses and dripped with sweat, she confiscated the supplies and finished bandaging him.

"I don't recommend wearing a prosthetic," she said. "Not until you've healed a—"

"Get me a prosthetic," he insisted between panting breaths. "It'll come in... handy."

She narrowed her eyes. "I do not appreciate your warped humor right now."

Maybe not, but his warped humor was needed. By them both. As long as he had the strength to tease her, he wasn't in danger of dying, like the rest of her family.

Some of her tension lifted, proving his thoughts. Mumbling under her breath, she fit a sleeve over his mangled wrist, and secured one of his many robotic hands in place. One she'd custom built for him. In fact, he had multiple prosthetics for every appendage; the technological marvels had saved his life on more than one occasion.

"Please reconsider this. You're in no condition to—" she began.

But he cut her off, demanding, "Now." His steely tone allowed zero argument. "Take me directly to the Lords. No landing a mile away, so they won't see you wield your power." Long ago, Galen and Fox had decided to hide her ability, no matter the circumstances. He no longer cared about the ramifications. The time for secrets was over. Every second counted. "I trust them. It's time to show them what you can do."

"You might trust them, but I do not. They aren't your biggest fans. Me? They don't even tolerate. Plus, I don't like the company they keep. Gods and goddess, Sent Ones, Harpies."

"Do it for me. Please," he said. He hustled around the room, weaponing up. "You might not trust them to help me, but trust that they'll help Leila."

Before the army had arrived, she'd looked at Galen with something akin to awe, as if she found him worthy of her time, her life...her heart. He wanted, *needed*, to see that look again. And he would. Soon. Cronus would pay dearly for taking Galen's woman—he would pay with blood.

Fox's dark eyes glittered with all kinds of concern, but she offered a stiff nod, turned, and performed a complicated series of hand gestures, causing the air in front of her to sparkle. "The Lords moved to—"

"Explanations aren't necessary. Just get me there." He clenched and unclenched his metal fingers. Pain shot up his arm, every movement agony. Oh, well. "I will risk anything to get Leila back as fast as possible." Anything to save her from more abuse.

The sparkles intensified, nearly blinding him. Finally, another invisible curtain peeled back, creating a *Stargate*-like portal.

"I'll go fir—" Fox went quiet as Galen passed her. "Okay, then. I'll follow you."

He braced, ready for anything as he stepped through what looked to be a waterfall of liquid glass… Fox stayed close to his heels, two short swords in hand.

They entered a thunderdome of aggression.

The spacious room with metal walls had zero pieces of furniture. What it did have? Seven of the most violent predators in history. Though Galen had grown to trust these people, just as he'd said, survival instinct demanded he have a plan of action, in case someone attacked.

The two most notable threats? Hades, one of nine kings in the Underworld, and his eldest son, William the Ever Randy, who was cursed to die whenever he fell in love. The two immortals had fewer scruples than Galen, and more power than any being should have. How Galen envied their power…

He snarled. *Hate Jealousy!*

Hades could turn his body into smoke and ghost through an opponent. William could develop wings of smoke on command, and harm others worse than the wards at Leila's cabin.

To win a battle against the pair, Galen would have to fight dirty. Downright filthy, even.

"Welcome back, Galen," William said with a wink. "Maybe now the fearsome and mighty Lords of the Underworld will finally get the hysterectomies they so desperately need, and stop bitching about your absence."

He received a glare from Aeron, former keeper of Wrath and Leila's first love.

Sienna, current keeper of Wrath and the queen of the Greeks, occupied the space next to Paris, the keeper of Promiscuity. The two were never far from each other. Paris needed to have sex at least once a day, or he would weaken terribly.

Finally, the power couple. Keeley, the Red Queen, and Torin, keeper of Disease. With one touch skin to skin, the white-haired brute could ignite a world-wide plague. Humans died, but immortals became carriers of the virus. But with Keeley's help, he'd found a way to circumvent the process.

"Fox is a Gatekeeper. Interesting." Hades stepped forward, a tall, imposing figure, wearing an air of boredom as perfectly as he wore his suit.

"Sips, you fickle little bastard," Fox muttered.

Galen followed her line of sight and spotted the raccoon peeking over Hades's shoulder.

Sips shrugged, all *what can I say?*

The underworld king scratched Sips behind the ear and said to Fox, "I've always wanted a Gatekeeper on staff at Chez Hellfire. You and I have much to discuss." His tone was soft, even, but somehow more menacing than a blade. "However, now that our guests have finally joined us, we have other matters to address."

Guests? *Finally?* How had the group known Galen and Fox would show up? (Besides his hand.) "You can't have her. Not now, not later," Galen said, impatience buzzing in the back of his mind. "Legion is—"

"Missing. Yes, we know." Aeron spit the words. He was a big man with heavily tattooed skin, dark hair, and violet eyes—and Galen wasn't sure what Leila had ever seen in him. "You let someone abduct her."

Shame and guilt lacerated through his chest. *Never as good as the Lords. They succeed, I fail. They* deserve *to fail. They—*

That's enough out of you, Jealousy!

False Hope sprang into action. *Save Leila on your own. Be her hero.*

Bastard. The demon liked to urge him to place his faith in the wrong person, or the wrong action, so he became the architect of his own demise. Like a self-fulfilling prophecy, and a truly insidious evil. The fiend failed to comprehend that pride meant nothing to Galen. Only Leila's safety mattered.

"No one hates this situation more than me," he told Aeron. "Challenge me to a duel or whatever you wish, and we'll settle our differences once and for all. Just wait until after we've saved Leila. Legion."

"Honey," Aeron snapped.

No time for arguments. He clenched his metal hand once again and motioned to Fox. "Let's go. Open a portal."

"Slight problem," she replied, drawing another snarl from him. No more hold ups! "I was able to portal here because I put a tracker on Sienna the last time we were together." Everyone but Galen cursed. "I don't have a tracker on Cronus, or Legion. So. Anyone want to guess where he might have taken her?"

"Early this morning, the Goddess of Many Futures showed me two possible outcomes for Legion," Hades explained. "In one, she was abducted by Cronus. Which came as a surprise to me, considering Sienna had decapitated him."

The explanation came with a ton of baggage to unpack. "What happened after the abduction? What happened in the second future?"

Hades drew his black brows together, his dark eyes like never-ending pits of fury. "First, tell me how Cronus survived his beheading."

Do what's needed. Get to Leila. He nodded to Fox.

She said, "After Cronus escaped Tartarus, he mystically cloned himself." Tartarus, a prison for immortals. "The clone was programed to awaken upon his death, with a single mission. Find his soul in the afterlife."

Made sense. Souls could leave the spirit realm, but only if they had a physical form to inhabit. Aeron was living proof it worked. The Most High—creator of Sent Ones, angels, and humans—gifted him with a new body after his beheading.

"You should have told us sooner." Torin fronted on Galen, his hands balled, ready to swing.

Galen jutted his chin. "You can have a go at me after Aeron. Do me a solid and put a pause on your mantrum until Leilia is found."

Once, Torin had been his closest friend. And okay, yeah, Galen had maybe kinda sorta had a man-crush on the guy. White hair, black brows, pale skin, and green eyes...strength and cunning...a sense of humor even more warped than his own...

Yeah, if ever Galen had gone for a male, it would have been this one. Over the centuries, Torin had always been the friend Galen missed most of all.

If he could go back ...

No. He wouldn't change a thing. If his past had been any different, he might not have become the man Leila needed. He would endure *anything* for her.

William buffed his nails, all casual sophistication. A deception. An inferno raged in his baby blues. "If you're not coming up with ways to save Legion, do not speak. Yes, I'm talking to you, Torin. And Aeron. And everyone else. You do, and you'll lose your tongue. I'm pressed for time. Got a group of nerds I vowed to kill if they failed to perform a few measly tasks."

Whatever that meant.

Keeley jumped up and down, clapping. "Are you going to Hannibal Lecter them, like I suggested?"

Exasperated, William tossed up his arms. "Does no one listen when I issue a threat anymore?"

"I wasn't finished. Did I sound like I was finished?" Hades held up his hand, palm out, and every other occupant went still and quiet. "The goddess showed me who to recruit for Legion's search and rescue, as well as your arrival, and where we will find the girl."

Galen darted around Torin, closing in on the H-bomb. *Must proceed with caution.* Considering the amount of power the underworld king wielded, and as weak as Galen currently was, he couldn't afford to make a new enemy.

"Has Leila been hurt?" he demanded. "Do you know what's being done to her? Tell me!"

"Tell me," Aeron echoed, his voice broken at the edges.

Hades stroked the dark stubble on his stubborn jaw. "In one of the futures, she had bruises on her face, and a split lip. Whatever was done to her, she survived. In the other…she lost her head."

Chapter Ten

Fear iced Legion on the inside, while frigid winds iced her on the outside. Full body shudders wracked her. Her teeth chattered, her stomach churned with a mix of broken glass and acid, her mind whirled with all the terrible things these men could do to her. But more than that, she worried over Galen.

Had he gotten help in time? Or had he...

No! She wouldn't consider the alternative.

After Cronus and his army had dragged her out of the house, they'd taken her through a series of magical doorways. Not portals, not like Fox created, but smaller with a more turbulent pass-through experience; for just a second, as you stepped from one realm to another, rocks seemed to batter you.

Finally, they'd set up camp in a treacherous land with miles of snow broken up by the occasional ice mountain. Frost thickened the air. There was no sun, only a dark, angry sky thundering with displeasure.

The only source of light came from fire pits, where different animals roasted. Golden rays flickered here, there, chasing away shadows, but Legion wasn't sure which was better. The darkness or the light.

Someone had tied her hands behind her back and secured one of her ankles to a wooden stake. The rope offered little range of motion. No one had hurt her—yet. No one had helped her either, or even given her a coat. She still wore her tank top and shorts, her feet "protected" only by a pair of thin socks and lightweight tennis shoes.

Again and again she wondered how this had happened. How had she become a second-time captive? Terrified of drawing attention to herself. Bound by the whims of an unscrupulous king. Helpless.

No, not helpless. Not helpless ever again! Especially not now, when Galen needed her. Galen, who had spent hours with her, reminding her of the combat skills she already possessed.

Fear is an anchor. Cut the anchor and soar.

Or run.

Yeah, she'd go with Plan B. She scanned the camp. No one seemed to pay her any heed. Men bustled about, erecting tents and building more fires. No sign of Cronus. Legion turned her focus to the ground, searching for a possible weapon. Glittering icicles...more glittering icicles...there! A sharp one. She stretched out her leg, hooked the hunk of ice between her feet and dragged it closer.

After contorting this way and that, she was able to clasp the piece to saw at the rope. She had agreed to leave with Cronus, but she hadn't agreed to stay put.

A shadow fell over her, and she tensed, her gaze zooming up. Cronus! His muscular frame eclipsed the firelight. "Time for us to get to work," he said, crouching down so they were eye to eye. "I must warn you. My predecessor had a conscience. I do not. The true king needed to guarantee I would do whatever proved necessary to complete my mission."

Mission? Still sawing, as stealthily as possible. "What secrets do you think I possess?"

He reached out to sift a lock of her hair between his fingers. "Once, you lived in hell. Now you are a demon-human hybrid, who spent time in Lucifer's Palace of Infinite Horrors. You are the only person I know to escape and live."

A barbed lump grew in her throat as she recoiled. The Palace of Infinite Horrors—the site of her torture.

"Whatever you know about the layout of the palace, I will find out," Cronus continued, unconcerned by her emotional turmoil. "Even details you might not realize you possess."

"I know *nothing*. I was"—she shuddered—"blindfolded a lot."

"Doesn't matter. The mind is a labyrinth of knowledge collected by your senses. Or a puzzle, with different pieces scattered about. I have only to fit them together. But. To extract the information I seek, I must establish a mystical link between us."

Link... In other words, he must *invade* her mind. *Rape* her mind. "No!" She shook her head. "No, no, no." A thousand times no. "I won't let you do this."

"I do not need your permission." His tone was sharp enough to cut glass. "The more you resist, the more damage I'll do. Don't worry.

You'll hurt, but you'll survive. Though you'll wish otherwise. And if you wipe your memory, I'll return to Galen and finish the job I started."

Bluff! "You think I'd care? If I wipe my memory, I won't remember him."

He studied her more intently. "Do it, then. Wipe your memory."

Argh! Sawing, sawing.

Satisfaction oozed from the bastard. "Let us begin."

Sawing faster. The rope loosened just a bit, but not enough. *Come on, come on. Fight!*

He gripped her chin and commanded, "Look into my eyes."

She squeezed her eyelids tightly closed, still sawing.

He tightened his grip, and she cried out. Or tried to. Someone knelt behind her, wrapped a beefy arm around her neck, and constricted her airway. Though her chest burned, she resisted.

"Open your eyes," Cronus said, cajoling, "and I'll let you breathe. Won't that be nice? Filling your lungs. Think how good it will feel."

A finger brushed her knee, and her eyelids popped open automatically, without permission from her brain. Wait. Not a finger. Sips? Yes! The raccoon was here, in this frozen wasteland.

Had Galen and Fox come to her rescue?

Hope bloomed. Unless lack of oxygen had made her hallucinate? *Need to breathe.*

"Come now," Cronus said. "Peer into my eyes, Legion."

No. Never. But there was something about his voice...

Against her will, she slid her gaze to his...*Look away, look away.* Too late. His irises swirled hypnotically, snagging her as surely as a net. The hold on her throat loosened, and she inhaled deeply. Total relaxation poured over her, as warm as bath water, the frigid winds vanishing from her awareness. Cold, throbbing feet? No longer. Icy blood? No, oh no. Lava flowed through her veins.

Why had she fought this? *So nice.* No, so wonderful, just like Cronus, the man she hoped to please above all others always, always, always, and—

A sharp pain exploded through her temples, the feeling of relaxation subsiding, revealing a dark underbelly of menace. Insects seemed to crawl across her frontal lobe. She couldn't...she needed...

Footsteps, curses. Metal clanged against metal. The insects scampered out of her head, new pains cutting through her temples. Blood dripped from her nose. She blinked rapidly—*come on, focus!*

The icy tundra came into view, highlighted by those fire pits. Amid a soundtrack of war, chaos reigned. Men and women fought with savage determination. No mercy.

There was William the Ever Randy, laughing as he sliced a man from nose to navel.

Hades ripped out a man's trachea and tossed it to the ground, like garbage.

Torin and Keeley tag-teamed a group of six, tearing limbs from two opponents to beat the others.

Paris and Sienna sliced through the masses as easily as butter.

Aeron! Legion's heart raced, and tears obscured her vison. Oh, how she'd missed the tattooed warrior who'd once offered her a home, friendship, and a life filled with love and laughter. Why had she avoided him? Seeing him now, fighting so fiercely on her behalf, old resentments faded.

Then there was Fox, a woman maddened in more ways than one. She was fury incarnate as she spun, struck, spun again, struck again— Legion spotted Galen and whimpered.

He hadn't given himself time to strengthen and heal. He'd come for her.

Her heart raced faster. If Fox was fury, Galen was pure, unmanaged rage. He used his wings for both offense and defense. He swung his swords, punched, and kicked, all while hovering in the air.

Multiple men closed around him at once. On his next spin, metal hooks extended from the edges of his wings. Oh. Oh, wow. Those hooks disemboweled one victim after another. Guess Galen had replaced the razor blades with the thicker metal for maximum damage.

Metal glinted from one of his hands, too. The hand the soldiers had severed. A prosthetic?

His speed remained unmatched, bodies toppling all around him. He fought as dirty as a demon, but he had the heart of an angel.

He is mine. My man.

He hadn't just come for her; he'd risked *everything* to come for her.

In a rush of motion, Cronus moved behind her, yanked her to her feet, and placed a dagger at her throat. The tip pierced her hammering pulse. "Not another step," he told Galen.

Legion fought her terror and continued sawing, despite close proximity to her captor.

Panting, icy mist wafting in front of his face, Galen ground to an abrupt halt a few feet away. He wasn't the only one. Aeron came up beside him. William, Hades, and the others, too. Everyone but Torin, who picked off the remaining stragglers.

Finally! The rope fell away from her wrists. Legion reached up to grip Cronus's forearm, to push him away and ease the sting. He only dug the knife in deeper.

"Hurt her further, and I will make your torture my life's mission." Galen smiled, slow and all kinds of evil. "I'll enjoy strapping you to my table. Once I tire of your screams, your death will become a cautionary tale."

"You can have the parts I opt not to mince," William said to Galen. "Meaning you get nothing. I just ordered my Miracle Blade, and I'm excited to see if I can slice through a skull as easily as a tomato."

Cronus hissed and sank the knife deeper.

In unison, Galen and Aeron took a step forward.

"No closer," Cronus shouted. Considering the way his body trembled against hers, she suspected his panicked gaze was darting between the males. Unlike his creator, he had no real life or battle experience.

"Focus on me, Titan," Hades said as Sips leaped into his open arms. He caught the purring raccoon and stroked his back, channeling Dr. Evil, a fictional villain she'd kinda sorta crushed on during her stay in the cabin. "I am the one you should fear."

Cronus jerked against her, once again sinking the knife a little deeper.

She swallowed a gasp of pain, lest Galen and Aeron revolt.

"You've had plenty of opportunities to kill Lucifer," Cronus spat, "and yet you've failed. You allow the war to roll on, countless people dying for your cause. Why is that, hmm? You should tell your so-called friends the truth. As for me, I'll do whatever it takes to reclaim my throne. Something you should understand. Now, you have a choice. Chase after me, or save your demon girl."

With that, he jerked the blade across Legion's throat. Oh, the pain! Burning, stinging. Hot blood pouring. Vision blurring. Knees knocking, buckling. A whoosh of air as she dropped. Darkness encroached upon her mind, but not before strong arms banded around her, easing her fall.

A hoarse denial rang out, warm breath brushing the crown of her head. "You will heal from this, Leila. Do you understand? I've got you, and I'm never letting you go."

Chapter Eleven

Legion slipped in and out of consciousness. The first time she awoke, nearly mindless with pain, Fox was stitching the wound in her neck, and Galen was issuing commands and shouting obscenities at Aeron.

"Careful! Do not hurt her. Save her whatever the cost." Fury and fear layered Galen's voice. "Aeron, get out of Fox's way before I strangle you with your own intestines!"

"I don't trust your friend," Aeron snarled. "If she makes a play against my girl, she loses her head."

"*My* girl," Galen snarled right back.

"You're both children," Fox muttered. "Why don't you *both* get out of my way, hmm?"

When the needle pricked a tendon, a stream of searing agony sent a message to Legion's brain: *Total factory shutdown.*

Lights out.

When the lights flickered back on, sharp needle-like pinpricks stabbed every inch of her, deadened nerves regenerating. Icy cold invaded—shock?—and she shivered. She lay on her back, a soft mattress beneath her.

"Cold, sugar?" Galen's voice. "Let me warm you."

He lifted her legs and slid her bare feet underneath his shirt. The darling man was sharing his body heat, reminding her of a beloved hero in a Julie Garwood novel.

As Legion succumbed to sleep, she thought, *I think I'm in love.*

The next time she awoke, she was curled against Galen's side, their bodies covered by soft blankets. Or maybe his wings? Sweat drenched him. While her teeth still chattered from cold, he was clearly overheated. But he didn't seem to mind when she snuggled closer, basking in the deliciousness of his warmth and the decadence of his scent.

Drifting to sleep once again, she thought, *I'm* definitely *in love.*

Finally, she awoke for good and took stock of her physical condition. Only a mild twinge of discomfort in her neck. Not bad. She stretched, loosening knotted muscles.

Memories of Cronus's attempted mind-rape swooped in, but they were quickly overshadowed by memories of Galen's bravery and kindness.

Where was he?

Disappointed to find herself alone, she eased into a sitting position. A note lay on the pillow next to hers. She read: **Everyone is alive and well. Love, G**

Wait, wait, wait. Love? Had he meant it as a figure of speech? Or did he *love her* love her?

Excitement surged, but she tamped it down and kept reading.

PS: Now that I've saved your life—twice!—there's no better time to admit I also saved you all kinds of postage when I stole your letters from the cabin. You know, the ones you wrote but never sent. I particularly liked the part about how you'd never known true satisfaction until me. Let's discuss.

Ahhhh. The blood-soaked papers she'd seen under his clothing finally made sense. Maybe a normal response would be anger? Right now, she was just grateful he knew the thoughts that had been tumbling around in her head.

One thing was clear, at least. Galen wasn't nearby, and yet she felt hope for a better tomorrow. Therefore, False Hope wasn't responsible. And, now that she thought about it, she hadn't experienced any jealousy, either. Maybe his demons had no real power over her. Having lived in the presence of evil for centuries, she had better defenses than most.

Legion set the note on the nightstand and looked around. Sunlight glared through a large bay window, illuminating the entire bedroom. There was a desk with elaborate carvings, an armoire with crystal handles, weapons everywhere—swords, axes, and semi-automatics—and robotic birds positioned throughout. She recognized the floral wallpaper. Galen had brought her to the fortress owned by the Lords of the Underworld.

Even better, he'd carted her jewelry here. Everything she'd saved when those soldiers invaded her cabin. Darling man.

A fire crackled in a marble hearth, burning stalks of ambrosia like incense. Intoxicating smoke curled to the ceiling. As the drug of choice for immortals, ambrosia dulled pain and encouraged sedation. Kind of him, but she'd had enough sleep to last a lifetime.

She rose to unsteady legs and took a few uncertain steps, the metal bird at the foot of the bed clocking her every move. Alerting Galen?

The thought comforted her. Just in case he *didn't* know she'd awoken, she would text him. She opened the nightstand drawer, expecting to find her old cell phone. Hmm. No phone, but there *was* a huge box of condoms. *Flavored* condoms. Extra small. No way these came from Galen. So who had put them there?

A mystery for another day.

In the bathroom, she washed her face and brushed her teeth. Well, well. A glimpse in the mirror revealed her bloodstained clothing had been replaced by a pink T-shirt that read "Give Me Galen or—Just Give Me Galen!" and shorts with little red hearts.

In the drawer with an assortment of hair bows, tiaras, and brushes, she found another box of flavored, extra small condoms. Seriously. Who had stayed in her room?

Rushing footsteps echoed seconds before the bedroom door swung open. Galen strode inside, those gorgeous wings arching over his broad shoulders, and closed the entrance with a kick. His pale hair stuck out in spikes. A black glove covered his prosthetic. He wore a white T-shirt, the material hugging his biceps, and a pair of loose-fitting lounge pants. Casual clothing, yet he appeared anything but relaxed.

Familiar tension emanated from him as he crossed the distance and leaned against the bathroom door. Seeing him set off a chain reaction of sensation. First came heat, then tingles, then a flood of arousal. She hurriedly shut the drawer, hiding the condoms.

"How are you?" he asked, cautious.

Why cautious? "I'm better." Alive. If she had died without being with Galen—a time born of desire rather than anger, resentment, or revenge—well, talk about a true travesty.

"Are you pissed at me? For the letters, I mean."

"No. I'm glad you read them," she admitted. "And I'm glad you're here."

He regarded her warily as she approached and wrapped her arms around him. Was he, perchance, afraid to hope she meant the words?

"I missed you," she said, rising to her tiptoes. Her lips hovering over his, she breathed in his sweetness.

At first, he was stiff as a board, maybe a little confused. "Do you want to talk about—"

"No. I want to kiss you."

Relaxing, he gripped her lower back with one hand and cupped her nape with the other, the prosthetic. One yank, and her body was flush against his. Their groans blended when he crashed his mouth into hers and kissed her.

As he walked forward, she hooked her legs around his waist. He blindly reached out to fiddle with the knobs in the shower. Water burst from the spout in the ceiling, raining in the stall, creating a soft pitter-patter. Soon, hot steam turned the bathroom into a sultry dreamland.

"I want you. I need you," he rasped. "But what do *you* want, sugar? What do you need?"

"You." *Only ever you.* "All of you."

"Then all of me you shall have." He gripped the collar of his shirt and tugged, ripping the material. Then he gave *her* shirt the same snatch-and-go treatment. Cool air brushed her breasts, her nipples puckering. He groaned. "My glorious female."

She stepped closer, warm skin pressing against warm skin. Inhale. Friction. Exhale. Friction. Desire sparked, spreading like wildfire, burning her inside and out.

With his forehead resting against hers, he said, "If you're doing this to forget what happened or because you feel indebted to me...I'm okay with that. But next time, or maybe the fifth—or fifteenth time, I insist you want me the way I want you, or I'll say no. Probably."

She laughed, then moaned. "Too much talking. Kiss me."

Hand and gloved metal in her hair, he returned his mouth to hers. Their tongues thrust together in a wild dance. He urged her feet to the floor and tore the waist of her shorts, her panties. Yes, yes! Giving as good as she got, she shredded his soft cotton lounge pants, leaving him bare.

Galen. Bare. A sight she hadn't gotten to enjoy either time they were together. The first time, they'd been in a public setting, and in a rush. The second, Cronus had interrupted. Now, they were alone and well-guarded. She could do anything she wished...

Legion ended the kiss, needing a moment to drink him in visually. He was beyond gorgeous, probably the most beautiful man ever to live, with muscles galore, two butterfly tattoos on his chest—the perfect canvas for her tongue—and a wealth of bronzed skin.

Her gaze dropped, and she licked her lips. He was big. Huge. And her aching body was empty without him.

When he gripped his length, as if in offering, she licked her lips. *Magnificent.* Had any male ever been so seductive?

He gave her the same once-over, only slower, more thorough. His pupils swelled, swallowing his irises, making her adore the body she'd been given.

No. No male had ever been so seductive.

"The prosthetic," she began, only to release a keening noise when his knuckle circled her nipple. "Let me help you take it off." She would kiss the wound he'd sustained on her behalf.

"No need. The glove is waterproof." He stepped into the shower stall, taking her with him, hot water washing over them. "I can get it—and you—soaking wet."

"Mission accomplished," she whispered.

He gave her nipple a light pinch, sending a shaft of pleasure straight to her core. "You ready for more?"

"With you? Always." An undeniable truth. A *shocking* truth.

Before she could fist his massive erection, he spun her around, putting her back to his chest. He lifted her arms and flattened her palms against the tiled wall. "I want you *more* ready."

She expected intense sexual play, with his big hands kneading her breasts. Man and machine working together. Barring that, she expected him to thrust his fingers inside her, and go straight for the gold. Instead, he gently shampooed and conditioned her hair, then soaped her up from top to bottom, his touch perfunctory. Letting her become accustomed to each new sensation?

"I'm ready," she said, and groaned.

"Not enough."

Maybe *he* needed to be readied. She turned to face him, snatched up the soap and cleaned *him.* Remaining perfunctory wasn't an option. She *worshipped* his body. Wasn't long before little growls rumbled in his chest.

"You don't follow any rules but your own, do you?" he rasped. "I am the same."

"I'm glad."

Without warning, he spun her once again, forcing her back to rest against his chest. This time, he fit his erection in the crack of her ass. He nibbled on her earlobe, cupping her breasts. While both his hand and the prosthetic kneaded her plump, giving flesh, the prosthetic applied a little more force. The variation drove her wild.

Anticipation buzzed along her nerve endings, and she wondered what he would do next.

"More?" He glided a hand down, down her stomach, and circled her navel.

"Yes, please." Reaching back, she tangled her fingers in his wet hair.

He continued to knead with the prosthetic, kicking her feet apart and using his other hand to thrust two fingers inside her. Immediate pleasure. She cried out, her back bowing.

The heel of his palm pressed against the center of her need, every inward glide sending a new bolt of frenzied passion through her. He made love to her with those fingers. Thrusting deep, so deep. In and out. In and out. Going slow, so agonizingly slow. No longer just driving her wild—driving her to the brink of madness.

"This first time," he said, "I'm going to make you come hard and fast. I'm going to take the edge off, and give you a taste of all I'm offering." He ran the shell of her ear between his teeth. "But it's not going to be enough. It's never going to be enough."

Pressure built, bliss consuming her bit by bit. She panted harder, writhed with more force, and tugged on his hair, awash with sensation. "Galen."

"More?" he asked. Still kneading, still pinching. Still thrusting his fingers in and out, in and out.

Then he wedged in a third finger.

She came in a rush, a strangled cry leaving her, inner walls contracting. Bright, beautiful stars winked through her vision, her mind snagging on a single word: *yes, yes, yes.* Her galloping heart banged against her ribs. For a moment, her lungs hitched, breathing impossible. Then she was panting again, drenched in Galen's scent. No. *Their* scent. Wildflowers, dark spices, storms—sex.

Hard and fast? Check.

The strength leached from her muscles, and she sagged against him. Good thing he kept his strong arms banded around her, keeping her upright.

"Good?" he asked, his tone rough, ragged, and strained.

"So good." But he was right. It hadn't been enough. New fires erupted, pressure building all over again. Hunger turned ravenous, another cascade of warmth pooling between her legs. "Are *you* ready for this, Galen?"

"Yes," he hissed. He dipped his finger into her core, as if he needed another hit of her wetness. As if she were a drug.

"Not enough," she said, mimicking him. Determined to make him as mindless, she whirled around. She kissed down his chiseled torso...licked his butterfly tattoos, exactly as she'd imagined. The mystical ink heated against her tongue.

"You don't have to do this, sugar."

"I know." On her knees, she peered up at the spellbinding male through the thick shield of her lashes. "You're mine, so I *get* to." With her hands on his hips, she leaned toward him...closer...and licked the slit.

Lids heavy and hooded, he threw back his head and bellowed with pleasure. His neck muscles corded, the tendons extending. Stretching out his arms, he pressed his fists into the stall walls. Water sluiced over the butterflies, every ridge of strength, and into the golden happy trail that led to his massive erection. *Magnificent beast.*

"Leila," he croaked.

"If I do something wrong, tell me." She gripped the base of his shaft. "I've never done this before." Not willingly.

"You don't have to—" he said, trying again.

"Mine," she said, and swallowed his length.

She was clumsy at first, but she didn't care. *He* didn't seem to care. He hissed and growled and clawed at the wall. Soon, a fervor took hold of them both, nothing more important than his climax. She licked, she sucked.

A roar escaped him, and it was then, in that frenzied slice of life, that she recognized the full brunt of her power over this man. As strong as he was, she was stronger, because he lived to make her happy.

The knowledge emboldened her. He was hers. This moment was hers.

"Don't want to come in your mouth," he rasped. "Not this time."

Agreed. She wanted to know his taste, wanted to experience everything with him, but this first time, she wanted his shaft buried deep inside her when he came.

Legion stood to wobbly legs. Galen swept her into his arms, carried her out of the stall, and eased her onto the bed. The kiss of cool air on her water-damp skin made her shiver anew. But Galen quickly warmed her up, his tongue like a flame as he licked his way down her body. He laved her nipples, teased her navel, and grazed her inner thighs with his teeth.

Shallow breaths left her. Had anything ever felt this good? He nipped a path closer to the heart of her desire.

"Yes," she pleaded. "Do it."

The width of his shoulders kept her legs spread wide, leaving her vulnerable to his every whim—and glad for it.

Warm breath caressed her inner folds as he smiled at her, a slow curl of his lips. "You're soaked for me."

"Desperate," she admitted.

"All this honey...all mine."

"Yours."

Liiiick. A scream ripped from her soul. Galen. Devoured. Her. She reached up and back to grip the iron headboard. He thrust his tongue inside her. Again. And again. Wave after wave of rapture crashed over her. When his fingers joined the fun, Legion thought her mind might break from the pleasure. Lick, thrust. Suck, withdraw. Nibble, thrust—two fingers this time. Three.

Yes! Sensitized from head to toe, she came again, this climax more ferocious, the pleasure almost unbearably intense. Harder. Faster. And more wondrous.

"Need inside you," Galen said, his voice more ragged than ever before.

"Inside! Now."

"Going to give you everything." He jolted up, smashing their mouths together. Their tongues rolled and clashed in a sensual battle, the pleasure undeniable, extending her orgasm. She moaned.

Hooking an arm underneath her knee, he spread her legs farther apart and poised his shaft at her opening. Then he paused, panting. She paused, too, her panting breaths a mirror to his. Their gazes met, currents of electricity arcing between them.

A bead of sweat trickled down his temple. "I am what you want? You are sure?"

"Beyond a shadow of a doubt."

He slammed inside her.

Yes, yes! She screamed, a third climax sweeping her up, up, consuming her body and soul.

Galen pounded in, slid out. In, out. Good wasn't an adequate word, she decided. Sublime? Closer. Perfection—ding, ding, ding.

"Galen." She locked her ankles over his backside, clinging to him, wanting his body to experience the same sublime pleasure.

"The things you make me feel…" Inhalations labored, he gripped the headboard, using it as leverage. Pounding harder, faster. Ensuring she felt him in every cell. Euphoria glittered in his eyes. "I'm so close already."

She arched her back and nipped his chin. "Kiss me."

Frantic now, he lowered his head, melding his mouth to hers. His shaft continued to move in and out. Faster and faster, shaking the entire bed, making the headboard rattle. Pictures tumbled from the walls and shattered on the floor. Neither of them paid any heed. In, out. Even faster. In, out. Waves became a tsunami of sensation. A rapturous gale force.

She lost herself in the moment, in the man. He threw back his head to roar at the ceiling, coming in a white-hot rush. She let go, falling into another climax…

And even more deeply in love.

Chapter Twelve

Galen's heartbeat had yet to slow. He cradled Leila against his naked body, chest to chest, the softness of her curves conforming to the hardness of his strength. One wing stretched underneath her, while the other covered her. He surrounded her. Every time he breathed, he drew in more of her luscious scent.

Never, in all his endless years, had sex so consumed him. The world could have crumbled and he wouldn't have cared. Nothing had mattered but Leila's pleasure. She'd come alive, her passion a torch that had nearly burned him to ash.

The perfect way to go.

Their first time, he'd experienced a measure of contentment. A shock, yes, considering they'd had sex in a bathroom. But the contentment had not compared to this. This...

This was unlike anything he'd ever known. Part contentment, part exhilaration, with satisfaction and genuine hope for a better future. This was the life he'd always dreamed of having, but feared he couldn't achieve. This was what he'd *needed*. A mate who valued him.

He realized he would rather be with Leila than rule a thousand worlds. As sappy as it sounded, she completed him. Spending every day together wouldn't be enough. He coveted more time with her, and he couldn't blame Jealousy.

That didn't stop False Hope from taking a swing at him. *The Lords will grow to hate her—because of you. They'll never forgive you for what you did in the past. They might pretend otherwise, but hate will always infect their hearts. The longer Leila remains with you, the higher the likelihood you'll ruin her life. She'll resent you. Eventually, you'll lose her.*

Galen would rather *die* than lose her. *Fight the rise of panic.*

She petted his chest, saying, "The demons acting up? Telling you we're destined to split, maybe?"

"How did you know?"

"They are trying to convince me to part with you. But I know they are liars, and so do you. We just need to do the opposite of whatever they suggest, and prepare for amazing results."

The opposite of accepting hatred from the Lords—fighting for their love. Galen couldn't control how they felt about him, but he *could* control how he treated them, and whether or not he let go of past grievances.

He kissed the corner of Leila's mouth. "Thank you."

"Anytime." Her blunt-tipped nail glided over his nipple as she traced an X on his pec. "This time was better than the first, right?"

The hint of vulnerability proved utterly adorable. "What we just did was better than *any* time, ever. I've never stuck around after sex, never wanted to encourage another go 'round, or wanted to imprint my essence on another person. Now, I think I'll throw a very manly he-fit if you try to bail."

She snickered, delighting him. He'd feared this latest abduction would break her, tainting her recovery, yet she had a new zest for life.

"I can do anything," he added, 100% serious, "except let you go."

"You *can* do anything. Over the years, you could have killed more Lords. You didn't. You could have won more battles and wiped out all the Lords at once. You didn't. You could have killed Ashlyn when you kidnapped her. You didn't. Because you never put your whole heart into the war." She thought for a moment, then gasped. "You *liked* fighting the guys, didn't you, so you had an excuse to remain in their lives?"

An astute observation. One he'd never allowed himself to consider, even when he'd walked away from battles he'd known he could win. He'd only ever told himself that every villain needed a hero, someone worthy of his skill, or eternity would get very boring, very fast.

"Once," he said, "I might have been a closet good guy. No longer." The things he'd done... the things he would do if anyone hurt his woman... "Do you hope I'll morph into someone like Aeron, who adheres to a strict moral code?"

"I like you just as you are." Voice soft, she said, "Do you hope I'll morph back into the tempestuous girl you knew before?"

"Of course not. I like you just as you are." He would take her however he could get her. But the woman she was now? The one who melted when he touched her? He liked her best of all. "I hope you'll grow to like you as much as I do."

"Wait. Why wouldn't you change me back into someone fierce and fearless?"

"Don't get me wrong. I liked that girl, too, and admire her sass. And I think she still exists inside you." Every so often, he caught a glimpse of her fire. "But she desired Aeron, which is a total deal breaker for me. The woman in my arms is smarter. Obvi. She chose to be with me. And she's stronger than you think. She fought to survive a bleak situation. Twice! But the icing on top? She knows my past, yet she still looks at me as if I hung the moon." He got high on that look.

She met his gaze, and he sucked in a breath. There it was. The look of adoration. An-n-nd yes. Instant high.

Hard as a rock, he cupped her nape and urged her closer for a soft, lingering kiss full of languid heat and wanton desire. When he considered sliding into her a second time, a realization dawned, and he cursed. "I didn't wear a condom."

Her eyes widened, and she sat up, crossing her legs, her breasts bobbing. "So I could end up pregnant. A mother... I've never considered having a child. Have you? Wait. You have Gwen." Brow furrowing, she said, "Why do you have a scrapbook about her life, but ignore her in reality?"

A clench in his chest. "Her life is easier without me in it. If I sought a relationship with her, I would only drive a wedge between her and Sabin."

"I think she's capable of managing a relationship with both of you, the same way *I'm* going to manage a relationship with both you and Aeron. So how about you give her a choice in the matter?"

Jealousy frothed, ready to pounce. Leila and Aeron? *I'll die first!*

Galen ignored the demon, and the fury. He scrubbed a hand down his face. "Once upon a time, I worked with Rhea, Cronus's wife. She knew about Gwen before I did and though we were allies, she sought the girl's destruction. How much worse would my enemies attack if they knew I loved her?"

"Gwen can take care of herself. Plus, she has the Lords." Leila drummed her nails against her knee. "Did Rhea help you create the Hunters?"

Hunters—an army of humans who had believed Galen was an angel. At his orders, the men and women had fought to eradicate immortals and their "evil" from the world. All the while, he'd laughed that they'd had no idea they worshipped the evilest immortal. "She was imprisoned in Tartarus for centuries, but yes. Until her escape, she used mortal advocates."

The things they'd done together...

Ignore the guilt. Guilt would only weigh him down.

Leila traced a fingertip over the sheet. Hoping to appear nonchalant? "Would you be upset if I was pregnant?"

"I...wouldn't," he said. Shocker! But he'd spoken the truth. A chance to be a father, and part of a legit family...to have an eternal tie to the woman he loved...the idea appealed to him greatly. "Until we've gotten things straightened out with Aeron and the others—and Cronus, and Lucifer—we should be more careful."

Disappointment sparked in her eyes, but she nodded. "You're right. I know you're right. I mean, we haven't even talked about whether or not our relationship is exclusive."

"We just discussed having a baby. We're exclusive. However, since Aeron came up, you should know that he and I have some unfinished business."

"About me?"

He gave a clipped nod. "We're in the middle of a multifaceted argument."

When he offered no more, she sighed and prompted, "About?"

Why not admit the truth and gauge her reaction? "I want to be with you, and he wants to gut me. I want to keep you always, and he wants to separate us. I want to continue breathing, and he wants me to stop."

Her shoulders rolled in, the reaction he'd expected but had hoped he wouldn't receive. "Promise me you'll talk with him, like a gentleman, and not hurt him."

Once again, fear rose up. Here it was, proof that he would lose Leila if he couldn't make things work with Aeron.

Looked like he would be letting go of past grievances and focusing on the future, after all. Otherwise known as handing the Lord his balls, with a *thank you, sir, may I give you another?* "I will promise, if *you* promise not to be alone with him. And I reserve the right to protect myself from a deathblow."

She stiffened, grating, "You don't trust me not to cheat with a married man?"

"I don't trust *Jealousy*. The demon will fray my control."

"Sounds like an excuse." She hmphed, but also petted his butterfly tattoo, as if to soothe him before Jealousy struck. "But I agree to your terms. So. Go on. Practice your gentlemanly speech. Pretend I'm Aeron."

"All right, I will. While most humans like to picture their audience naked to keep from getting nervous, I'd rather pluck out my eyes than imagine this particular audience unclothed. So, we'll switch things up. You can picture *me* naked."

She chuckled as he untangled his body from hers. Then he stood at the side of the bed, giving her full frontal access to his rising erection. Feminine approval colored her cheeks, and she fanned her face.

Sign me up for more of this.

"Well, hellllll-o, handsome," she said, and wiggled her brows. "But, uh, how am I supposed to use my imagination when you are actually naked?"

He stroked his length up and down. "Oops. My bad. Should I put something on?"

"Don't you dare! Now let's hear that speech, so I can have my wicked way with you."

Want that. Want her. He cleared his throat with exaggerated force. "Aeron," he said in the kindest voice he could manage. "I'm here today to humbly request you back the fuck off. The end."

Leila covered her mouth in a failed attempt to mask her smile.

He arched a brow. "What do you think? I know, I know. The middle is too long and needs tweaking. And I wasn't sure about my use of *humbly*. Or *request*."

Pouting, she said, "You didn't list any of the reasons you're attracted to me. Or how perfect I am. Or how you revere every inch of me."

He gave his length another stroke. "How about I give you every inch of *me*?"

Temptation made flesh, she leaned back, reclining on the pillows. "Yes. Remind me how perfectly we fit."

Awareness charged the air. Smile slow and languid, he placed his hands and knees on the mattress, one after the other, and crawled up her lush little body, thrilling when goose bumps spread over her inner thighs.

"Would you like an oral presentation first, or hands-on instruction? Never mind." He licked the heart of her need, earning a raspy moan. "I mentioned I like to multitask, right?"

* * * *

Though resplendent with sexual satisfaction, Legion was a bundle of nerves. She toyed with her diamond choker, but the jewelry failed to comfort her. It was then that she realized she hadn't wanted jewelry when Cronus had taken her; she'd wanted Galen.

He and Fox stood sentry in front of a large window, watching as she paced from one side of the entertainment room to the other. A massive plasma screen occupied an entire wall. A leather couch scattered with beaded pillows and forgotten popcorn kernels formed a half moon around the coffee table, a million game controllers scattered there. A trash bin overflowed with empty beer cans and broken bottles of wine.

On the walls were different paintings of the Lords, each one more hilarious than the last. Clearly they'd tried to outdo each other with the ridiculousness of their outfits and poses. A thousand magnets covered the mini-fridge door, everything from Care Bears to an ad for erectile dysfunction. At the small, round kitchenette, a blowup doll sat in one of the chairs.

Home sweet home. How she'd missed these people and their warped senses of humor.

The door flew open, startling her. Aeron stalked inside, his eyes narrowed. His hands were fisted, but he wasn't carrying a weapon, so Legion considered it a win.

Aeron was a stunningly beautiful man. Not Galen beautiful, but then, *no one* was Galen beautiful. Even better, the tattooed warrior had a heart of gold underneath that bad boy exterior.

"Aeron." Heart galloping, she raced over and threw herself into his waiting arms.

He swung her around, then set her on her feet and pushed her behind him. Confused, she peeked around him…ah. Okay. Galen had crossed the room and now stood a few feet away. *His* eyes were narrowed now, his hands fisted.

He warned me. She moved between them, her arms outstretched. "I don't want you guys to fight. Please, don't fight." How was she supposed to make the two most important men in her life get along? Especially when her boyfriend carried the essence of jealousy, and his "competition" was her first love, the man she'd given up everything to be with.

Aeron ran his tongue over his teeth. "You like him?"

"Yes." Very much. But she loved him, too. Not that she was ready to admit her feelings to everyone. First, she had to get her new life in order.

In hell, her abusers had killed her spirit. Now, thanks to Galen, she had been revived.

"Tell me why," Aeron insisted. "Why him, and no other?"

"Yes, Leila. Tell him why," Galen prompted, his tone devoid of emotion.

Okay. *Let's do this.* "No matter how much Galen despised me for my actions toward him, no matter how furious he's been with me, he has always desired me. Me, and no other. He's always excited to see me, even if I only leave a room for five minutes. He thinks I'm perfect just the way I am."

Galen's expression began to soften.

"He's a thief and a liar. A betrayer." Aeron reached for her, but she sidestepped him, her stomach flip-flopping. "He can't be trusted. He destroys everything he touches."

Now Galen laughed. She heard pain, but no hint of amusement, and it ripped her insides to shreds. He'd made mistakes. A lot of mistakes. But so had she. So had Aeron. He'd paid in blood. It was time to forgive.

"You're right, Aer-bear. I can't be trusted, and I destroy everything I touch." Galen's baby blues slid to Legion. He no longer resembled the fun, sensual warrior who'd rocked her world. Here, now, he was the merciless villain capable of any dark deed. "He's right. I lied to myself. I won't let go of the past. I lied to you. I won't just defend myself from an attack. If he attempts to keep you from me, I will kill him. *No one* keeps you from me."

Allowing Jealousy to rule him? She lifted her chin and squared her shoulders. The past few weeks, Galen had been strong for her. Today, she would be strong for him.

"He can't keep *me* from *you*," she said. "And if he tries, you won't have to strike at him, because I will have already mowed him down."

Pride sparkled in Galen's eyes, and maybe Aeron's, too.

"I want you both in my life," she continued. "I've been deprived of enough already, don't you think? So find a way to get along. That's an order."

Fox stepped forward. Planning to threaten Aeron?

"No." Legion pointed a finger at her. "You don't have a say in anything."

The other woman returned to her spot beside Galen.

Well, well. Legion hadn't possessed this air of authority in forever, and she liked it. "Galen, tell Aeron you're not going to lie to him ever again."

"I won't lie unless—"

"Galen," she snapped.

"I won't lie," he said, and sighed.

"Aeron," she said next. "Tell Galen he's welcome in your home."

Aeron remained stubborn. "He killed one of my friends."

"Yes, and your friend came back to life," she reminded him.

"After thousands of years," he retorted.

She glared. "Tell. Him."

Like her boyfriend—she really liked that title—Aeron sighed. "Fine. He's welcome here."

"Good boys." With a contented smile, she patted Aeron's cheek, then kissed Galen's lips. "My work here is done." Head high, she strolled from the room.

Chapter Thirteen

"Legion!" "Honey buns!" "Honey badger!"

The chorus rang out as different Lords and Ladies noticed her arrival in the kitchen. At the table, Keeley sat on Torin's lap, feeding him grapes. Paris stood behind Sienna's chair, massaging her wings and shoulders. Sabin occupied a window alcove, watching as Gwen paced in front of him.

Everyone rushed over to hug Legion. She was all smiles as she returned their embraces.

"You look so good," Keeley said. "You're glowing! I knew Galen would be an incredible lover. I just knew it."

Torin cringed, saying, "My poor, sweet ears."

Legion's cheeks heated. "Sometime in the future, I would like to speak with you alone, Keeley." There was too much going on right now, too many prying ears. She had questions about Cronus's mental link—ways to stop him if ever he or anyone else tried again. As old as Keeley was, as much knowledge as she possessed, she would know.

"Are you going to ask me for sex advice?" the other woman asked. "Because I've been thinking about this for the past two minutes and I have some ideas."

No time to reply. Gwen whisked in front of her. "Okay, I need you to blink twice if Galen forced you to look so happy so we wouldn't gut him."

Galen's daughter was a stunningly beautiful woman. Harpy. Whatever. She had long, strawberry blonde hair, big blue eyes so like her father's, and flawless golden skin. Adorable iridescent wings fluttered on her back.

Harpies descended from demons and vampires, and they were

extraordinarily strong and as fast as lightning. By nature, they were bloodthirsty, vicious, and vindictive.

"I'm genuinely happy," Legion said, her smile widening. "Your dad is a good man. He loves you, you know. I think you should give him a chance."

"Ew. Gross." Gwen grimaced. "You said the D-word."

"You tamed the untamable Galen." Sienna pushed her way forward, using her wings to nudge people out of the way. "From now on, I'm going to call you The Legiondary."

Keeley was the next one to step up. "I'm so jealous. You've got Galen in the sweet spot—desperate for your approval. Never let him leave it."

Legion fluffed her hair.

Footsteps sounded. All conversations ceased. Excitement crackled in the air.

Heat pricked the back of her neck. Galen had followed her, hadn't he?

Slowly she pivoted on her heels. Sure enough, he loomed in the kitchen entryway. His ocean water blues scanned the occupants, and to an untrained observer, he might appear cold and removed. Not Legion. For a split second, his gaze hitched on Gwen, glittering with untold longing.

The same untold longing consumed *Legion*, blending with all the love in her heart. So much longing and love it terrified her. Would she always feel this strongly with Galen? And what would happen if ever she lost him?

"Hello, traitor," Sabin said, his tone even. He unveiled a smile full of bite, and yet, there was no real malice, as if he wanted to hold on to a grudge he'd already forgiven.

Still, anger sparked. Lashing out might not be such a bad thing.

"Hello, *son*." Galen's smile had bite, too, but just like with Sabin, there was no malice. He spread his arms and waved his fingers. "Come give Papa a kiss."

"How about I give you a full-on make-out session with my fists?" Sabin lunged at him.

In a flash of movement, Gwen had her boyfriend—husband—consort—*whatever* on the floor, her boot positioned on the back of his neck. "Nope. No fighting. I don't like blood on my appliances."

One day, I will be swift and strong. She would train until nothing and no one had the ability to overpower her. She would protect Galen the way he had protected her.

"Where was this animosity the last hundred times I visited?" Galen asked casually.

With Gwen crushing his windpipe and all, it must have been difficult for Sabin to speak, but somehow he managed to rasp, "You weren't sleeping with our girl back then."

"*My* girl. And anyone who says otherwise gets—" Galen looked at Legion, popped his jaw. "A ten-second frencher. *Not* a dagger through the heart."

"A frencher is worse," Paris said, and pretended to gag.

"Me, me!" Keeley raised her hand. "Sign me up for some of *that*."

A growl reverberated in Legion's chest, surprising her. She loved Keeley, and knew the woman would never cheat on Torin, so why—

Ahhhh. Okay. Yeah. The demon of Jealousy. Legion finally had something to lose, so she'd finally gotten a true taste of the bastard's evil, despite her natural defenses. No wonder Galen hadn't wanted her to spend any alone-time with Aeron.

Her winged warrior offered her a sensual wink. "Look at me, being a big boy again. I didn't attack, even when I had every provocation. Do I get a reward?"

"Big boys get big rewards," she said, and blew him a kiss.

"If you'll excuse us." Galen took Legion's hand with his metal one and led her from the kitchen.

No one protested. A few people wagged their brows. Keeley tried to high-five Gwen, who flatly refused, so the Red Queen high-fived *herself*.

"Did anyone else find Galen hot just now?" she heard Sabin say. "Oh, uh. Yeah. Me neither."

She snorted. Galen rolled his eyes, but he couldn't mask his contentment.

When they reached a private hallway, he spun to face her. No, not just to face her, but to back her into a wall. With his hands at her temples, and his wings wrapped around her sides, he caged her in.

Heart racing, blood heating, she peered up at him. "Hallway quickie?"

He brushed the tip of his nose against hers. "I want to prepare you," he said.

"And I want you to prepare me, too." Arching her hips, rocking against his erection, she kissed the thundering pulse in his neck. "Can we go to our bedroom first?"

After hissing in a breath, he said, "I'm not talking about sex. Though we'll get to that. I want to prepare you for the truth. I'm going to mess up sometimes. Being nice to people who threaten me is new, and I'm asking—no, I'm begging—you for a learning curve. I realize now that I might have been too *hopeful*"—he sneered the word—"when I promised not to attack your loved ones."

"*Our* loved ones," she corrected. He wanted a family, and she wanted him happy. So she would do everything in her power to help him patch up his fractured relationships. "And maybe I was too ambitious, asking you to always stand down. Besides, it's not like these Lords and Ladies can't protect themselves."

He blinked with surprise before gifting her with his most wicked smile to date, his gaze promising untold sensual delights. "If I didn't think our crowd of eavesdroppers would peek around the corner and watch, I would drop to my knees right here, right now."

The erotic glint in his eyes… Shivers and heat spread through her. She placed her hand over his heart—his *racing* heart. As much as she wanted him, he wanted her right back.

Aeron rounded the corner, spotted them, and sighed. "We have a location for Cronus. Let's go. I called dibs on the killing blow, of course, but you can pulverize his bones or feast on his organs afterwards."

Wait, wait, wait. All of the strength she'd acquired seemed to vanish in an instant. Suddenly queasy, she dug her nails into Galen's shoulders. He was heading off to war already?

Anticipation glimmered over his expression, and worry bombarded her. If something happened to him…

Galen placed a swift kiss on her lips. "We have unfinished business, Sugar Tits. I'll be back, and we'll pick up right where we left off. Count on it."

She snort-laughed, and her eyes widened. Still this man had the power to amuse her during the most stressful times of her life.

He's strong. He'll come back to me.

But what if he didn't?

A lump grew in her throat. "Be careful," she said, forcing herself to pry her nails from his body.

He gave her another swift kiss before striding off with Aeron, side by side, the two arguing over who got to make that last, killing blow.

A lone white feather floated to the floor. She bent down to pick it up, and traced the tip over the seam of her lips. So soft, so warm. Scented with her man's unique fragrance. A true comfort.

After pinning the feather underneath her bra, she returned to the kitchen. Realizing she wasn't alone, she screeched to a halt. Fox had remained behind, and now sat at the table eating a sandwich.

"Why aren't you with Galen?" Legion asked. "Shouldn't you be opening a mystical doorway or something, and guarding his back?"

"William wields magic. He opened the doorway. I don't...I can't..." Fox frowned and grabbed hanks of her hair.

The demon of Distrust acting up? "You don't have to worry. William won't strike at Galen, because hurting Galen would hurt me."

Eons ago, William had lived in hell. As the adopted son of Hades, he'd had a kingdom of his own. Until he was cursed by a witch, and prophesied to die at the hand of the woman he loved. Now he spent his days trying to decipher a book of codes, strange symbols, and text that might or might not explain how to save him.

He lived by no moral code but his own, but it was as warped as Galen's sense of humor. Still, anyone he'd liked—and there were only a handful of names on the list—he'd stringently and violently protected. As a part of the Lords' family, Legion qualified.

Fox inhaled deeply, exhaled sharply, and eased her hands into her lap, as if concentrating on the conversation took great effort. "You're right. I should be with Galen, guarding his back. But he messaged and told me to stay here to protect *you*." She paused. "You're going to be the death of him. You know that, right?"

"No." Legion shook her head and clutched her stomach. "I would never—"

"You won't mean to, but you will. Look at the wives of the other Lords. All strong. All capable of protecting themselves and their loved ones. But you...you are a burden. Galen is forced to protect you, leaving himself open to attack."

The blood rushed from Legion's head, her ears ringing loudly. Fox wasn't wrong. Her fears had made her a weak link. An anchor with the potential to drag him down—to drown him.

So what was she going to do about it?

* * * *

Galen rushed down a narrow, underground corridor, Aeron at his side. Water dripped from limestone. Glowworms emitted a bright phosphorescent light until they detected the sound of heavy breathing and the rumble of footsteps.

Darkness worked better for today's ambush, anyway.

A musty scent tinged the cool, damp air. How he missed the sweetness of Leila's wildflowers.

Focus. Right. He needed to figure out what Cronus wished to acquire from Lucifer's Palace of Infinite Horrors, and fast.

"Betray her," Aeron said as they turned a corner, "and I'll remove your balls with a machete."

Galen snorted, ignoring a new surge of jealousy. He knew Leila would die for Aeron. *Will she live for me?* "You'd use any excuse to touch my balls."

"Children, please." William ran a few paces behind, practically crackling with eagerness. "It's not nice to argue in front of friends...without first letting those friends take bets about who will win."

Their group turned another corner, and all banter ceased. The corridor shrank, restricting Galen's wings. Despite the pleasant temperature, sweat sheened his skin.

Cronus doesn't know you're here. You'll surprise him, take him out, and all will be well.

False Hope, attempting to build him up. Foreboding bombarded Galen. If the demon claimed the Titan king had no idea the Lords had arrived, the opposite was true. "Cronus knows we're here," Galen said. "He's expecting us."

"How do you know?" Aeron demanded. "Did you both attend the same Villain 101 course? So far, we've found....let me count...zero traps, and killed all of the guards we've come across."

Constant doubt was oh, so fun. "He's never let himself be seen before. Why now, unless he has plans?"

"So what do you suggest?" Aeron asked. "We'll kill him whether he knows we're here or not."

They snaked around another corner, and finally came to an abrupt stop. Row after row of armed soldiers blocked the path, semi-automatics aimed.

Boom, boom, boom! The army opened fire, bullets blazing through the cave. Galen jumped in front of Aeron. A sharp pain tore through his shoulder, gut, wing, and thigh. Searing agony. Blurry vision. Ringing ears. Blood gushed from each wound.

Taking an injury meant for someone else? *That's new.*

Strength drained from him in a hurry, and he dropped. Bonus: he avoided the next line of fire. Using his momentum to his advantage, he rolled forward, kicking two soldiers between the legs and coming up swinging. His short swords cut through their torsos. Intestines spilled out, the splash-splash blending with bellows of shock and pain. With a simple twirl of his wrists, he struck again, removing their heads.

From the corner of his eye, he saw William take down six men at once, all with a swipe of his smoke-wings. The men clawed as their faces as flesh melted from their bones.

Note to self: Stay on William's good side.

As Galen fought his way through enemy ranks, he took out the soldiers causing the most damage to his...allies. Maybe they'd be friends again one day, maybe not. Animosity was easy. You never had to worry about being vulnerable or betrayed. But as Leila had taught him, caring for others came with boundless rewards.

Bodies fell around him. Sensing a presence behind him, he spun. Just in time. He got to watch as Aeron took out two soldiers who'd snuck up behind Galen, planning to decapitate him.

"Now we're even," Aeron said.

"Did you take a bullet for me?" he asked, battling a soldier of his own. Thrust. Parry. "Then no. No, we aren't even."

"Anyone see Cronus?" Sabin shouted.

"No." "Nope." "Got too much of someone else's blood in my eyes."

Very few of the Titan's soldiers remained standing. Galen grabbed one of the last by the throat and squeezed hard enough to compromise the guy's windpipe. "Where is your leader? Tell me!"

"Don't..." The victim beat at his arms unsuccessfully. "Know."

"Then you're of no use to us." He didn't waste time with a proper interrogation or torture. He squeezed harder, until the man had strangled to death, his head lolling forward.

Disgusted, Galen released him, letting him crumple to the rocky ground. Panting, knees a bit weak, he scanned the cave. The rest of his team finished off the remaining soldiers.

"Everyone all right?" Aeron asked between panting breaths.

"Barely," Galen muttered.

The others sounded off. There were a ton of injuries to contend with, but no one had died, so all was well. Leila would be happy. And maybe Galen was happy as well. It was nice, having men he'd once considered brothers protect him rather than attack him.

Before his legs gave out, he made a big show of sitting on the ground. "Let's take a moment so you wimps can rest."

William tossed him a handful of bandages. "Dress your wounds before you bleed out. None of us want to listen to a lecture from Legion."

"She doesn't lecture," he said, even as he accepted the offering. "She cries and emotionally rips out your guts."

"Oh. In that case." William tried to reclaim the bandages.

Galen batted his hand away, growling, "Mine."

Snickering, the warrior ruffled his hair. "Look at you. So possessive of your Band-Aids. Reminds me of young William, when I was just a lad in my mid-hundreds. Keep this up, and you'll be one of us in no time."

Chapter Fourteen

A gaggle of voices drifted from somewhere down the hall. Had everyone returned?

Anticipation vibrated in Legion's bones. She stopped stroking her array of bracelets and rushed out of her bedroom. Down the hall. Down a winding staircase. Only a few hours had passed, but her worry had only grown stronger. And dang it, she'd missed Galen more than she would have missed a limb.

The voices increased in volume, so she knew she was on the right track. Mid-way, she ran into Olivia, Aeron's wife.

Olivia had a fall of dark, curly hair, the perfect contrast for her pale, pale skin. To this day, despite everything she'd witnessed with the Lords and everything she'd endured in her quest to save Aeron from demon assassins, her sky-blue eyes watched the world with innocence and optimism, two things Legion had never possessed.

As a Sent One, Olivia had first been a Messenger, who was later promoted to a Warrior, a (supposedly) mad, bad, savage killing machine whose only mission was the slaughter of demons. But because Olivia had developed feelings for Aeron, she'd chosen to fall from grace instead of kill him, leaving her home and family to be with him.

At one time, Legion had despised her for it. *I thought I wanted Aeron all to myself.* Boy, had she been wrong. She'd never really desired him, had she? Not sexually, at least. She'd hero-worshiped him, the first man to ever show her kindness. She'd craved his affection, not his touch. She'd yearned for his attention, not his body. With Galen, she wanted everything, nothing held back.

Never had she been more grateful for the sweet and generous Olivia, who was everything the tormented Aeron had needed. Just as sarcastic, edgy Galen was everything Legion needed. He was ruthless, relentless, and driven, qualities that had kept her from losing herself to the past.

"Legion!" Olivia grinned, and they embraced. "Sorry, sorry. I mean Honey. I'm so happy to see you."

"I'm so happy to see you, too. And I'm good with either name. Truly!" Inside, she knew who she was, no if, ands, or buts. She was Leila, plain and simple. But that particular nickname was reserved for the man who'd gifted her with it. Him and him alone.

"Things are going well with Galen, then?" Olivia asked, no judgment or censure in her tone.

"Oh, yes." Legion beamed. "He can't get enough of me."

"Who can? You are a treasure." Olivia kissed her forehead. "And I'm glad you've found your person. Your happiness is our happiness."

Overcome by a wave of affection, she gave the Sent One another hug. "Thank you. For everything. You are a wonderful woman. Now come on. Let's go greet our men."

Together, they jolted back into motion, picking up the pace to soar through an open doorway, entering the war room.

Aeron, William, Gwen, and Keeley cuddled together, whispering. It was a heated exchange. Torin, Sabin, Paris, and Sienna were cleaning their weapons to store in a large, metal armory, discussing Cronus. Apparently he hadn't attended the battle royale.

Every single one of her friends was splattered with blood. Where was—

There! Her heart careened out of sync. Galen was shirtless—her favorite look on him, well, besides from his total nakedness look—with several bandages wrapped around his torso. His leather pants were ripped, revealing bandages on one of his thighs, as well. He wore more blood than the others.

Seeing him wounded and bloody...white-hot rage crashed over her, crushing any hint of fear. Cronus had hurt her man. The bastard's final mistake.

I'm going to kill him. He's going to die screaming.

Her nails lengthened and sharpened, converting to claws. The rage continued to heat, soon boiling, burning away the fears she'd carried for far too long. Old instincts surged anew, reigniting the viciousness that had served her well when she'd tormented souls.

Someone could hurt her? She dared them to try.

She might die badly? Better to go down swinging.

Galen had gotten hurt in a fight that should have been hers. *Never again.*

But she knew wars were not always won on a battlefield. Sometimes they were won in the mind. Before she made a move, she had to prepare the best plan of action. Namely, go by herself or recruit a team? If she invited one Lord, they would all insist on coming. As a group of testosterone-fueled cavemen, they had trouble with stealth, preferring a full-on tactical assault.

Cronus will rue the day he sought me out.

When Galen's gaze locked with hers, awareness crackled between them. Rage morphed into potent desire. She would handle Cronus— soon. Right now, she wanted to handle Galen, *all* of Galen, and celebrate his survival.

"Oh, my." Olivia fanned her face. "That look is hot enough to singe off my eyebrows."

"Leila," he rasped.

Without a beat of hesitation, she ran and jumped into his open arms. He hugged her close and spun, even enfolding her in the safety and softness of his wings while their lips crashed together in a fevered kiss. Desire electrified her nerve endings.

She distantly noted that other conversations had ceased. Or maybe they'd simply faded from her cognizance. Who cared? Galen's ambrosial taste intoxicated her, making her head swim and her body ache.

"Yeah, baby!" Keeley cheered, and there was nothing faded about it. Her voice boomed as if she'd used a megaphone. "Take it off and get it on!"

"Don't you dare make out with my daughter in front of me," Aeron grated.

Daughter. Yes. The title fit, like a perfect puzzle piece clicking into place. And in the name of daughterhood, Legion lifted her head, smiled at her adopted father, and proudly flipped him off.

Every female in the room burst into laughter. Some of the men laughed, too. Best of all, Aeron's tension evaporated.

"Galen is mine, and I'm keeping him," she announced. "You don't have to like him, but you will respect my choice. Actually, no. You do have to like him."

Galen's chest puffed up, though he tried to hide it. "I want you, Leila. I want to claim you now and always," he told her—loudly. "Say yes."

"Yes!" Pleasure tingled in her nerve endings. "Yes, yes, a thousand times yes."

"Have her back by ten," Aeron grumbled, "or I'll ground you both."

"Do you mean you'll grind Galen's face into powder?" Keeley asked. "Or that you'll cut off his wings, grounding him like a plane?"

Aeron nodded. "Yes. To both."

"You all suck." Galen carried Legion out of the room, kissed her once, twice, his tongue teaching hers a wicked duel. "You are the exception, as usual. You rushed into the room, eager to greet your man after battle. Walking wasn't fast enough."

"Well, I missed you," she admitted.

"You were concerned for my well-being, needed my arms around you as much as I needed to put them there."

"Never let me go." A plea straight from her heart.

"Never," he echoed. "Let me apologize in advance for bleeding on you."

His injuries! She gasped, horrified, and tried to wiggle down, but he only clasped her tighter. "Put me down so I can doctor you." She should have tended his injuries first thing *then* jumped his bones.

"I would rather die than set you down."

Frustrating, wonderful man! "If you continue to refuse, I might be the one to finish you off."

"Worth it," he said, and bent his head to nip at her lower lip.

"That is both romantic and foolhardy, Galen."

"Then we've hit the sweet spot in my wheelhouse, Leila."

Though she fought her amusement, the corners of her mouth curled up. "Listen, lover boy." She let the nickname linger in the air, then nodded. Yeah, it worked. "I need your energy and stamina to be on point today. You and me? We're gonna have sex, and you're gonna like it." Words she'd said to him once before. This time, they meant so much more. *He* meant more.

"I will love it." All coiled need and sizzling desperation, he intoned, "I will have you, all of you, and you will have every inch of me. With us, energy and stamina will never be a problem."

After entering her—their—bedroom, he kicked the door shut without missing a beat, then stalked to their private bathroom, where he eased her onto the counter.

"I need to see you," he said. When she held up her arms, he yanked off her shirt.

The ruby necklace she wore resettled in her cleavage. His gaze traveled over her body, then returned to her breasts, sheltered by a scrap of lace. Lace the same red as her jewelry.

"Exquisite," he rasped.

His pupils dilated as he cupped her, then kneaded the giving flesh. Beneath the lace, her nipples puckered for him, seeking his attention. He paid no heed to his bandaged injuries as he lightly pinched those distended crests.

Air hitched in her throat as she spread apart her legs to welcome him closer. Since he was already shirtless, his muscles and tattoos on magnificent display, they were skin to heated skin. Not close enough. Never close enough.

He was a killer, dangerous to everyone but her.

"You are the one for me," he rasped. "I'll have you and no other." Then he was kissing her, scattering the thoughts in her head. Only pleasure mattered.

* * * *

Galen divested Leila of her bra...her pants...her panties, leaving her in the necklace, and the necklace alone. Stopping their kiss was torture, but he did it, then stepped back to look his fill. Those glorious, bountiful breasts with their rosy tips. Curves for days and legs for miles. Between those legs resided the center of his entire world.

Hand and prosthetic resting on her knees, he pushed her legs even farther apart. So pink and pretty. *So wet for me, only me.* He claimed her mouth in another searing kiss, and plunged two fingers deep into her hot, drenched core.

Pleasure owned him. Owned her, too. Every time he scissored his fingers, she writhed and scored his back. *I've made her lose control.*

With pleasure came a new surge of desire—more!—the assault on his senses unparalleled. Necessary. He had her sweetness in his mouth, and her exotic scent fused to his cells. Her essence soaked his fingers, her inner walls clamping tight. Release beckoned, but he fought it, just as he'd fought to protect this precious woman from Cronus.

What greater cause could a man have than the safeguarding of a treasure?

The moment Leila had first entered the war room, he'd forgotten his injuries and the audience, losing track of the world. Had even lost track of the demons. He hadn't been jealous of anyone. There had been—was—no need. With Leila, he had everything he could ever want or need. And, for one of the first times in his life, he hadn't had to wonder about the legitimacy of his hope. He'd realized true hope wasn't accompanied by fear or foreboding, but peace. Such beautiful peace, as if light had chased away the darkness in his soul.

In this, the demons no longer had power over him. He and Leila had a bright future, because they were both willing to put in the work.

"Remember when I wanted to go down on you in the hall?" he asked, kissing a fiery path down her neck.

"Doubt I'll ever forget." Passion had roughened her voice, every word as potent as a caress.

"Time to make fantasy a reality." He dropped to his haunches. Cupping beneath her knees, he pulled her forward until her bottom rested on the edge of the counter. Her legs remained spread, her luscious core mere inches from his waiting mouth.

Peering at him, adoring him with her eyes, she leaned back, offering herself to him in supplication. "Do it." Not a request, but a demand. One he relished.

At the first lick, lust fogged his head and his muscles went taut. He had to stave off a sudden and fierce climax—he would last for his woman, would last as long as she needed.

"Yes! More, more!" She shook and moaned. "Pleeease, Galen."

Those pleas nearly pushed him over the edge, straight into the throes. "I understand the nickname now. Honey." He nuzzled her inner thigh, goose bumps rising up to greet him. Kiss. Lick. Suck. "I want your honey all over me. My greatest desire is giving you everything you need."

He licked again. Then again. He flicked his tongue over her little bundle of nerves before sucking harder. Then, oh, then, he thrust his tongue into her tight sheath, mimicking sex. She sank her nails into his scalp.

"Will never get enough of you." He feasted on her, wringing one…two…three orgasms from her body, until her breasts heaved with every breath, and her cries were incoherent.

Until he could withstand the agony and emptiness no more.

He jackknifed to his feet. She ripped at the fly of his leathers, freeing his throbbing shaft from its prison. Finally! Delicate hands wrapped around the base, squeezed, and stroked up, dragging a moan from deep in his chest.

He expected the worst of the throbbing to subside, or dull. Nope. Every sensation intensified.

"If I don't get inside you, I'm going to lose my ever-loving mind," he said between labored breaths. "You ready for me, sugar?"

"Beyond ready. Need you."

"You're aching for me, then?"

"Always."

A bolt of pride shot through him. Millions of men in the world, yet Leila desired him, and him alone. She trusted him with her body...and her heart? Maybe. She peered up at him, giving him the look, all adoration and hope, and he puffed up his chest. A common occurrence in her presence. But then, he had a woman other men envied. A *life* other men envied.

He reached out, opened the top drawer, and fished a condom out of its box.

"You're the one who's been storing condoms in my bedroom. But...they're flavored. And *small*!"

"They were a gift from Torin." He used his teeth to rip open the foil, then slid the latex down his rock-hard length. "He thought it'd be funny if I stopped to explain the condoms inside the box are actually extra-large. But they are. Extra-large. Probably XXXL."

She snickered, then he did the same.

He used the prosthetic to urge her forward. At the same time, he positioned the tip of his erection at her opening. Just like that, desperate need replaced amusement, and they moaned in unison.

"You are hot as fire, sweet Leila, and I long to be burned."

Their gazes met. Desire hooded her eyes, her irises wild. Passion-fever radiated from her flesh. Red, pouty lips were swollen from his kisses.

He leaned into her to nip that sweet lower lip—and thrust home. The muscles in his back pulled taut, the pleasure almost too much to bear.

She uttered breathy moans, enthralling him with her uninhibited abandon. "Galen!"

No woman had ever responded to him so fervently.

His legs began to tremble, so he flared his wings, using the feathery appendages to hold himself upright. Then…

Galen unleashed.

He pounded in and out of her, the carnality of her reactions fraying his control. Flushing skin. Trembling limbs. Racing pulse. Her breasts bounced, and her nipples grazed his chest. A sensual abrasion, like flint on steel, igniting a fire. Her hoarse cries rang out, a siren's song.

It wasn't pleasure that owned all the good, all the bad, and all the ugly in him, he realized; it was this woman. Whether she was the fiery vixen he'd first met, or the vulnerable beauty he'd rescued in the cabin, she was his, as if tailored to fit his every secret desire. He was her first, and he would be her last.

Exhilaration flared inside him, rapture. Wonder. He didn't deserve her, but he would not part with her, ever. Nothing and no one would separate them.

He ran her earlobe between his teeth, then licked her hammering pulse. Little mewling sounds slipped from her. Ravenous, he bit down on the cord of her neck. She jerked against him and screamed his name, inner walls contracting around his length, demanding their due.

The pleasure…the pressure building inside him…the rightness of the moment, his partner… Finally, he was home, where he belonged, with the one who owned his heart.

He made love to her mouth before lifting his head just enough to peer down at her. Light spilled over golden skin, illuminating her flawless beauty. One of his feathers had floated into her hair, the sight breathtaking.

Every part of me belongs to her.

Sweat dampened him as he increased his thrusts. Slam, slam. Heat collected in his testicles, soon shooting up his shaft…

"Leila!" Galen climaxed with a roar, his head thrown back. Hot lash after hot lash of pleasure jetted into the condom. He shuddered with rapture.

Finally, when the shudders died down, he sagged against her. She rested her head on his shoulder, trying to catch her breath. His own breaths were ragged, his throat raw from his bellows.

"That…that was amazing," she said.

"One of my favorite memories of all time." He removed the condom, tied the end, and tossed the latex into the trash bin. Despite his profound satisfaction and contentment, he was already hard again.

Holding her gaze, he dug through the drawer and withdrew another condom.

"Again?" she asked, and shivered with excitement.

"Again." After he'd rolled the rubber over his length, he framed one side of her face in his ungloved hand, traced his thumb along the rise of her cheekbone, and softly kissed her lips. "The appetizer was delicious, sugar. Now I'm ready for the meal."

Chapter Fifteen

Eight days of bliss. Galen and Leila stayed in bed, making love, talking, and laughing. But something major was bothering his woman, and he didn't know what, or how to make it better. He only knew his foreboding had returned and redoubled.

Many times, he'd caught Leila standing at their bedroom window, gazing out, lost in thought. Lost in *fury*, her body drawn as tight as a bow, her hands fisted. He'd asked what was wrong, had begged for answers, but she'd merely kissed and fondled him until he'd forgotten his name.

His Leila loved her pleasure, and he loved giving it to her. Loved when she gave it right back.

The demons did everything in their power to rile Galen up, but he refused to take the bait. He trusted his woman, not the fiends. Leila would tell him what was wrong when she was ready, and they would find a way to work it out. No other outcome was acceptable. Because, for the first time in his life, a true happily ever after was possible, all thanks to Leila.

In those eight days, other changes had come over her. Her fear? Gone without a trace. She smiled often, and always welcomed him into her arms, her bed. Sometimes he was the aggressor, sometimes she had the honors; they took turns. She slept deeply, nightmares no longer plaguing her. And now that he knew the joy of holding her as *he* slept, he couldn't fall asleep without her nearby. She was his peace. His family. His everything. He *belonged* with her, and to her.

Some days, she even joked with him. *We should clone you. One Galen to fight wars, one to clean our room, and seven others to see to my sexual satisfaction. I'm not sure you can keep up on your own, lover boy.*

He grinned, remembering, but the amusement didn't last long. He hadn't confessed his love yet. Even though he knew she loved him, too. She must. She'd started collecting the feathers he shed. But she'd made no mention of it, either, and he had a feeling the reason revolved around her fury, and whatever had sparked it.

That fury... he'd tasted it as they'd trained. The one responsible for it was going to die in agony, no doubt about it.

Leila's skill amazed him. The more she'd remembered her combat training, the more she'd taken him to the ground. In his defense, he'd been distracted by her breasts. And her legs. And her mouth. And every little noise she made. And the pulse that hammered at the base of her neck. Mostly, the smile she unleashed every time she succeeded.

Yesterday, Keeley had joined their session and shooed Galen away. He'd left the room, but had stayed nearby, listening to their conversation, telling himself he eavesdropped just in case his woman needed him.

"You mentioned you have questions for me," Keeley had said, "and I'm ready to answer."

"Cronus," Leila had begun, a quiver in her voice. "He invaded my mind. How do I protect my thoughts, my memories?"

Galen's stomach had twisted.

Keeley had made a little *hmmm, that's interesting* noise. "To invade someone's mind, you must establish a psychic link. Unless that someone has mental shields. To establish mental shields, you need practice. But I'll be honest. I'm surprised Cronus did this. A psychic link is the worst possible way to extract info from another person. You don't just see their memories, you feel the emotions they experienced. Why torture yourself in such a way?"

Did Leila still harbor fears, and she'd just gotten better at hiding them? Did she expect Cronus to find and harm her again?

Must find him first. Must stop him.

If Leila did fear another kidnapping, she didn't show it. Earlier today, she'd gone shopping with the other ladies, a few of the Lords acting as guards—for the mortals they came across. Gwen, her half-sister Kaia, plus Lucien's girlfriend Anya, the minor goddess of Anarchy, often acted like the emotional equivalent of children hopped up on caffeine combined with Disney villains.

Galen had remained behind, a difficult feat, even though he'd known Leila would be well protected. It was just...he wanted her to have normal experiences, like girls' day out. Fine. She'd told him to keep his ass at home so she could relax with her girls.

Now he lounged on a lawn chair beside Aeron, drinking ice cold beer on the porch, waiting for their women to return. Living. A ray of sunlight broke through a wall of gray clouds, a gentle breeze scented with pansies.

"You make her happy," Aeron said, sounding resigned.

"I know. But she does the same for me." He just wished they'd made headway with Cronus. So far, there'd been no more sightings or whispers from spies. Galen had his best people searching. "I will take care of her for all eternity, this I swear to you."

A pause. A sigh. Then, "I believe you."

His chest clenched. "I don't deserve your trust, but I thank you for it. And though I can't regret the past that brought Leila and me together—yes, you uncouth tyrant, that's how you say it—I'm sorry for the pain I've caused you over the eons."

Another sigh. "You are forgiven. We've all done things to hurt others."

Clench. "Not to complain but…this forgiveness would have been nice days ago."

"Days ago my female hadn't given me an ultimatum. Forgive you for real and for good, or sleep on the couch."

Galen winced, as if embarrassed for him. "You are so whipped."

An SUV with blackened windows sped up the drive, screeching to a stop in front of a massive marble waterfall. The girls had returned! He leaped to his feet and rushed down the winding stone pathway.

"Yeah, I'm the whipped one," Aeron called.

Without turning, Galen lifted a hand to flip him off. The vehicle's back door opened. Leila spilled out, bags dangling from her hands. *Oh, yes. I'm whipped.* She wore a black leather halter top and a very short mini-skirt; he had to wipe away drool.

As soon as she spotted him, adoration lit her expression. The look he loved and craved. It made him remember the early days of his life, when he'd believed every life mattered and redemption was possible. But even still, his sense of foreboding kicked up a notch. She might be adoring, but tension thrummed from her, stronger than ever.

Bags jumbling together, she ran over and leaped into his open arms. "Guess what?" she said, making him forget his doubts. "Keeley told me I'm not pregnant, that I won't have a kid for another couple of years.

Only when we're good and ready."

Disappointment and relief mixed, an odd sensation. "Doesn't mean we should stop practicing."

"Agreed."

He turned and strode past a wealth of roses growing along wrought-iron trellises, closing in on the fortress, a structure both tall and sprawling, with two side towers and copper steeples. Ivy covered several stone walls. Around the border, amazingly detailed stone statues of men and monsters stood sentry.

As Galen carried his woman through the front door, Aeron called, "Hello to you, too, Legion."

She winced. "Sorry, Aeron. Didn't see you out there."

Galen sent a mental F-U to Jealousy, and the demon whimpered.

Leila pressed a swift kiss to his lips. "Wait till I show you what I bought."

"Something sexy?" he asked, nearly undone by the thought.

"Something *suuper* sexy. Spoiler alert. The G-string is going to drive you wild...when you wear it while dancing for me."

* * * *

I have to do this, and you have to let me.

The words whispered through Galen's mind, accompanied by the *tick tick tick* of a bomb nearing its detonation. Drowsy but alert enough to know his woman wasn't in his arms, he rolled over and reached for her, intending to pull her close. Cold sheets greeted him. *Tick tick.*

He frowned. Blinking open his eyes, he sat up. Bright light streamed through the window, illuminating pink walls, and the framed oil painting she'd hung yesterday. In it, Galen posed like someone named George Costanza. Whoever that was.

Yesterday, Leila also strung twinkling Christmas bulbs around the four-poster bed, and decorated the mantel with stuffed road kill she'd dressed in doll clothes.

"They had terrible ends," she'd said. "Hopefully, this tribute honors them."

He'd grinned then, and he grinned now. Her whimsical style appealed to the boy he'd never gotten to be. The boy he'd always *wanted* to be.

No sign of her, or even the clothes they'd scattered over the floor last night. *Tick, tick.*

"Leila?" he called, refusing to worry.

No response. *Tick, tick, tick.* He kicked his legs over the side of the bed. His feet sank into the plush carpet as he stood. Cool air brushed his bare skin. Naked, he rolled his shoulders and stretched his arms over his head. His wounds had healed completely, no longer complaining when he moved.

Shaking out his wings to leave feathers on the floor, he strode into the bathroom. *Tick.* The walk-in closet. *Tick.*

Was she in the kitchen, eating breakfast, maybe? He'd zapped all of her energy last night.

He grinned. After making love for hours, her urgent moans teasing his ears, they had snuggled lazily in bed. Unlike before, Leila hadn't traced Xs over his pec as they'd basked in the afterglow, waiting for their bodies to calm.

His grin vanished. *Tick, tick.* Why the lack? Last night, he'd been too exhausted to ponder the reasons. Now he wondered what thoughts had rolled through her mind.

She realized she's better off without you. She—

Enough!

Tick tick. Galen hurriedly brushed his teeth and dressed in...Well. They certainly weren't his clothes. One of the Lords must have snuck in, stolen all his clothes, and replaced them with a T-shirt that read "My Father-in-law likes Liver, Fava Beans, and Chianti," a pair of too-tight leathers, and combat boots chopped up to look like flip-flops around the toes.

A warm tide of contentment flowed over him, momentarily drowning out the ticking bomb. The Lords of the Underworld only played jokes on their friends. The bigger the joke, the more they cared.

Galen owed Leila a debt he could never repay. For this, and so much more. She had brought him to this point, doing the impossible, giving his heart new life. She'd taught him how to love—how to live. She'd reminded him just how much trust and loyalty mattered, how valuable they were. How rare. She'd shown him the importance of creating bonds with others.

One of the first lessons he'd learned in combat was the importance of having backup. His instructor had said, *Think of every soldier as a string. Tie two...three...four of those strings together, and each one benefits. Each one is strengthened. The more strings grouped together, the harder it is for a foe to cut or fray one, much less all.*

Who didn't like being stronger?

Friendship-wise, Galen had reached everyone but his daughter. Any time he'd tried to converse with her, she'd stomped from the room. Last night, at Leila's urging, he'd left out the scrapbook he'd made. All he could do now was wait and hope for the best. And he did. For the first time, he believed he could have the best, that he and Gwen could get to a good place. One day. If he could win over the Lords of the Underworld, he could win anyone. He just had to fight for what he wanted, never conceding defeat.

A sudden realization rocked him. If he had managed to kill Lords during their war, he wouldn't have their friendship now. If he had killed Aeron specifically, he wouldn't have met Leila. He wouldn't have a family, or a chance with Gwen. He would have missed all this, and more. He would have missed the life he was meant to lead.

How close he'd come to losing everything, to disqualifying himself from a perfect fate, and he hadn't even known it.

His earliest instinct had been correct. Lives were worth saving, worth *redeeming*. Even his. Even those he'd once resented. With one small caveat, of course. Anyone who threatened or harmed Leila, well, their life was forfeit, as good as gone; they deserved what they got.

Needing her enfolded in his arms, he made his way out of the bedroom. A robo-bird flew in front of him, hovering, a piece of paper trapped within its beak. A love letter from Leila? The grin returned, only to fall as he read the text.

My darling Galen,

I am in total and complete love with you. I'm sorry I never told you to your face. I was going to reveal all when I presented you with a gift (more on that in a sec). But, just in case something happens, I decided to confess now. I don't want you going through life not knowing how I feel.

You mean so much to me, and I want to protect you the way you've protected me. I WILL protect you. You asked me what's been bothering me lately, and I'm ready to tell you.

I've been thinking of ways to off Cronus, and finally I know. So, I'm going after the king of the Titans.

Before you freak out—please don't freak out. I've got this, lover boy. I won't even have to do any tracking. I just have to leave the fortress so he can find me without worrying about dealing with you Lords. (Yep. YOU are a Lord of the Underworld. A fearsome warrior loved and adored by the others. They would so die for you. They'd complain about it constantly, sure, but they'd still do it.) I've noticed the ease you guys have with each other, and it's made me happy.

Please don't come after me. Let me come to you—with Cronus's head. (My gift to you! (Happy birthday, Merry Christmas, and Happy Anniversary for eternity!)

I'm sorry I didn't stick around to discuss this with you in person. I knew you'd try to talk me out of it, or even take measures to stop me. But I have to do this. He hurt you. No one is allowed to hurt you. You have given me so much. I don't know if I can ever convey the absolute joy of knowing I'm the one who gave you contentment after you waited multiple lifetimes. Me! In return, you didn't just give me back my life, Galen. You became my life.

Love,
Your Leila

The ticking bomb finally exploded inside Galen. He balled the paper in his fist, ragged growls rumbling in his chest.

I have to do this, and you have to let me. The words Leila must have uttered before she'd left him sleeping in bed.

Another snippet of remembered conversation followed. Before they'd fallen asleep, she'd asked, *Do you know what Cronus wants from Lucifer's palace?*

No. Do you?

Maybe? There have always been rumors about the palace. See, Lucifer likes to steal spirits of the dead—spirits who belong elsewhere. He keeps his favorite captives in a private realm, and only he has the key. That key is supposedly bespelled—to look at it is to forget it. Supposedly. What if Lucifer stole the spirit of Cronus—the original Cronus—from the prison realm that is earmarked for Pandora's demons? If Cronus 2.0 gets his hands on Lucifer's key, he can find and free Cronus's spirit. Body and spirit can merge, ensuring the Prince of Darkness can no longer contain the king of the Titans.

A body was a spirit house, so to speak. When the house crumbled, the spirit was forced to move on to a spirit realm. And there were many such realms. The one in the upper level of the heavens, of course, and the one in the deepest pits of hell. But as Leila had said, there were also prison realms for those like the Lords of the Underworld and Cronus, the former keeper of Greed.

As much as Leila had trained, Galen should have known she

planned to go after Cronus. Panic roiled inside him, and the demons pounced, emboldened.

Going to lose her. Might be too late already.

No. No! She was smart, wily, her training at the forefront of her mind. She could survive anything.

She wanted to do this alone. Too bad. While she'd learned to trust herself, she hadn't learned to trust others. And he understood, he did. In the heavens, he'd done the same thing. The thing was, she didn't *need* to do this alone. They were a team, and he would forever have her back.

Galen charged into the hall, shouting, "Aeron! Fox! William! Gwen!" Their names scraped his throat like razors. His daughter might not like him, or want anything to do with him, but she was a trained killer, and he wanted her expertise for the most important mission of his life. "Get your weapons, and get your asses in gear. We're going hunting."

Chapter Sixteen

Two soldiers shoved Legion to her knees directly in front of Cronus. The king of Titans settled on a throne of skulls.

She was exactly where she'd hoped to be. At his mercy. *Do not smile.*

She had no room for fear, not anymore. Fury had overtaken her.

Careful. Must appear weak, afraid, and non-threatening.

How strange. For so long, she'd dreamed of being strong, invincible. *Check, and check.* Dreams did come true. If she was going to walk away from this battle, however, she needed this man to gravely underestimate her.

Mere hours ago, she'd wandered around the castle district of Budapest, as if lost. The day before, she'd *strolled* through the castle district, happy. She'd wanted Galen at her side, but she'd needed his absence so she could sell her most valuable jewels to pay for an ancient sword her friends had mentioned.

Metal wings protruded from the hilt, and the blade had been forged by a Sent One. The perfect weapon for Galen.

The sword would arrive at the fortress tomorrow. *And I will be there to watch his face light up when I present it to him.*

Today, she'd wanted Cronus's guards to come out of hiding and ambush her. They hadn't disappointed. She'd had no weapons on her, because she'd needed none. Not then, not now.

Look at me, so easy to defeat. Take what you want, your majesty...I dare you.

"Leaving the Lords was foolish, and you aren't a foolish woman," Cronus said. "So why did you do it?"

He'd taken over the realm that Rhea—his ex-wife—had owned.

Well, Rhea had owned it before Cameo, keeper of Misery, had soundly thrashed her and left it abandoned. The realm's crowning glory was this open, airy temple constructed with ancient stones. But there were other treasures to be had here. Trees with leaves as colorful as butterfly wings surrounded the outer walls, the scent of ambrosia heavy in the air. Precious gems were scattered over the ground like pebbles, glittering in sunlight.

Once Legion had killed Cronus, she would take ownership of the realm.

A head for Galen, a realm for me. For us.

At least a hundred soldiers were positioned around the temple's perimeter. Men she would offer a choice: *Let me go, or die.* Just a matter of time.

Not yet, but soon. In the corner stood ten winged warriors, each bound by chain. These particular Sent Ones had white and gold wings, which meant they were Warriors. Though they were upright, their eyes were closed, as if they were asleep. Magic crackled in the air around them.

How had Cronus captured them? Even unconscious, they projected an aura of malice and determination. The second they escaped, they would try to tear the Titan limb from limb, no doubt about it.

Would they throw mantrums when they discovered Legion had already killed the male?

In that moment, she regretted not bringing Galen. They could have done this together, could have fought side by side. They could have *protected* each other. She'd just...she'd wanted to prove she could do this on her own.

"I asked you a question. Do not make me ask again," Cronus spat, backhanding her.

Pain exploded through her head, and blood filled her mouth, coating her tongue with the taste of old pennies. He wore spiked rings. At least he hadn't stabbed her. Two short swords were strapped to his back. He even had garrote wire wrapped around his wrist, and two daggers sheathed at his waist. Also a dagger at each ankle.

Galen liked to weapon-up in a similar manner. Had the clone copied him?

Here goes. She spit out the blood and did her best to make her voice weak. "I needed to speak with you. You hurt Galen so bad...*so bad.* He hasn't recovered. If I give you what you want, will you leave him alone?

Please." *Too much?* "You don't have to search my memories. I'll tell you everything I remember. Just leave Galen alone, okay?"

Cronus smiled with cold calculation, the very reaction she'd craved. "What's to stop me from *taking* what I want, hmm?"

"Honor? Integrity? Actually, you *can't* read my thoughts." False Hope had taught her well. How to use the power of suggestion. How temptation and greed could be roused in men, immortals and mortals alike. How to build someone up…then tear them down. "I have shields now. Good ones." Truth. She'd worked with Keeley. But she had no desire to use those shields.

The king drummed his fingers together, and she knew she was close to hooking him. "If I want in, you won't be able to keep me out."

"You're wrong?" She posed the words as a question rather than a statement. Pretending to be afraid, she stood, as if she meant to run. The guards stationed at her sides pushed her back down with enough force to rattle her brain against her skull. *For that, they'll die with their king.* "I *can* keep you out. And I will. Unless you agree to my deal."

Don't agree, Cronus. Come on. Force your way in…

He slid to the edge of the throne and leaned toward her, his eyes narrowed. Well and truly hooked now.

Triumph flared, reminding her of the glory days, when torture had been the only item on her To Do list. *Shouldn't smile.*

"Look at me," he commanded, placing his hands on her temples.

"Not until you agree to my terms."

"Look," he grated.

Again, she pretended to be afraid. Slowly, she slid her gaze to his. As soon as their eyes met, fingers began to crawl through her mind, sorting through her thoughts. She offered no resistance, her memories his for the taking. And take he did.

"You have no shields," he murmured, smug. Triumphant.

Her insincere cries for mercy only encouraged him. When he found what he was looking for—the Palace of Infinite Horrors—she almost laughed. She gave him full access to the memories—and all the emotions that came with them. The fear. The humiliation. The degradation. The pain. The helplessness. The desire to die.

He jerked his hands away from her, severing contact. Too little, too late. Powerful emotions couldn't be wished away. With a groan, he pulled at hanks of his hair.

"Enjoy the memories with my compliments," she said, and rammed her fist into his nose.

Cartilage snapped and blood spurted, his next groan replaced by a bellow. She wasted no time, clasping the hilts of his daggers and stabbing him in the throat. A quick jab, jab, jab. More blood. Warm wet splattered over her face and hands, but she didn't slow. She hacked through skin, muscle, and tendon until his head held on by a single thread of tissue—then she cut that, too.

As head and body disconnected, she realized she'd done it. She'd won! And yet... the victory left her hollow, because Galen wasn't here to share it with her.

Her earlier realization solidified. Yes, a thousand times yes, she should have talked with him, should have told him all her thoughts and plans. She'd given the man her heart and her body. Why had she denied him this?

Never again, she vowed.

Murmurs rose behind her, the guards rallying, preparing to do battle with the one who'd slain their king.

They choose to die, then. Very well.

She turned—and caught sight of Galen. He wasn't alone. He'd brought Aeron, Gwen, Sabin, Fox, and William, too. Armed for war, the group rushed through a portal. They took in the scene with a swift visual sweep then positioned their body in front of Cronus's soldiers, blocking her.

When a guard raised his sword, Galen *tsk*ed and said, "Trust me. You don't want to do that."

Happiness swelled within Legion. He'd come for her!

"Galen, look!" She swooped down, tangled her fingers through Cronus's hair, and lifted the severed head high in the air. "Look what I did!"

He blew her a kiss laced with relief, amusement, and joy, a heady combination. "I'm so proud of you, sugar."

To her astonishment, the chained Sent Ones awakened a second later, their eyes popping open. In unison, they stepped apart, splitting down the middle to reveal a *third* clone of Cronus. Oh... crap. He wore a white toga, and just as many weapons as his predecessor. Unlike the Sent Ones, he wasn't chained.

"Another one?" Aeron bellowed.

"I've *got* to get a clone of myself," William remarked, not the least bit fazed. "Finally! I would have my perfect mate."

Legion stomped her foot, aggravated. Why wouldn't the Titan just die already?

New Cronus—NC—opened his eyes, and scanned the temple. "Attack!"

The guards sprang into action, swinging swords and spears at her friends. Knowing they could take care of themselves, she chucked the severed head at NC, nailing him in the face. He staggered backward.

In her periphery, she noticed Fox had stopped fighting the guards. Someone made a play for her throat, but Galen fended him off. Fox continued to stare at the Sent Ones, her gaze solid black. Black lines appeared beneath the surface of her skin, too, branching over her cheeks, down her neck. Like poison. At the same time, the ends of her hair caught fire, yet never burned.

That's new. Thanks to Distrust?

The Sent Ones remained as still as statues, but rage boiled in their eyes. Steam might have wafted from their nostrils.

Oh, yeah. Cronus had definitely used magic to hobble the warriors.

"I can keep Cronus inside the temple," William called, his voice strained as he gutted three soldiers, one after the other, "but only temporarily. Whoever wants the honors needs to kill him quick."

Legion returned her gaze to Galen, who swung his sword, removing a soldier's head. He nodded at her. "Do it, sugar," he said, trusting her to take care of the big bad.

Chapter Seventeen

Shell-shocked but utterly mesmerized, Galen killed the Titan king's guards one after the other by rote, watching as Leila went on the offensive, attacking the newest version of Cronus.

Magnificent creature. Blood splattered her skin. She was dressed to kill in black leather, displaying a skill and viciousness he admired. She used the daggers, her fists, legs and elbows, every part of her body a weapon. Whenever necessary, she ducked or dove out of the way.

Having just awakened from a however long slumber, Cronus 3.0 had slower reflexes. He fought back, of course, even landing blows, but he took a lot more hits than he landed.

"Hurt my man? Hit *me*?" Leila flung the accusations at him. "I. Always. Repay." She punctuated each word with a brutal jab of the dagger. First, his heart. Then, a kidney. Then, his liver.

Still the Titan continued fighting, unsheathing his short swords. He wielded the blades with tremendous skill. Once...twice...a dozen times, Galen had to stop himself from closing the distance and ending the battle. *Hurt my woman, and suffer.*

He managed to resist the temptation, grounded by pride. Leila projected zero fear as she blocked. No, she was the epitome of fury, determination—and joy.

Cronus didn't know it, but he'd lost the war the second Leila found her confidence.

"Can't...hold..." William grated. He stood with his arms outstretched, his features strained as he powered the invisible barrier around the temple, preventing Cronus from flashing away.

"No worries. I've got this." Leila evaded Cronus's next kick. She went low, spun, and came up swinging the daggers. Yes! The blades slashed the Titan's throat. Blood poured as he stumbled back and gasped for breath he couldn't catch.

Galen grinned. Payback hurt.

When she dropped a second time, she swiped out her leg, knocking the king's feet together. Too weak to right himself, he toppled. Impact jarred the male. Merciless, Leila straightened and executed another kick, then another, until he lost his grip on both swords. Only then did she jump atop him.

Once again, he backhanded her, splitting her lip before she could deliver the final blow. A woman on a mission, she worked to maintain her perch, then leaned down...and bit into his already savaged neck, her teeth tearing out part of his trachea.

Galen knew the power of that bite, and the accompanying venom, and rejoiced. Soon, Cronus wouldn't have the strength to rise, much less strike her again.

White foam collected at the corners of his mouth, his motions slowed. Leila pressed her booted feet into his thighs and her knees into his shoulders, lifted her arms, and struck. Her daggers hacked at his neck.

That's my woman.

Tendons, muscles, even his spine was severed. Even when Cronus stilled, she continued. Blood spurted in every direction, soon coating her arms, dripping from her fingertips. Jab, jab, jab. Finally, the head detached from the body. An injury no immortal could recover from.

The blood-drenched daggers dropped from her trembling hand. Galen wanted to pound his chest with pride. Around him, Gwen, Sabin, and Aeron plowed through the soldiers with lethal precision, thinning the herd. Bodies and parts piled up around them.

Fox worried Galen. She was making her way toward the Sent Ones, attacking anyone who got in her way, even her allies. Every few steps, she paused to shake her head, clearly at odds with the demon of Distrust.

Two guards came at Galen from behind, their pounding footsteps heralding their approach. He flared his wings and spun, the metal hooks slashing their throats.

"No, Fox!" Sabin shouted. "Don't do it!"

Galen spun again, preparing to rush over. Except she needed no protection. The *Sent Ones* needed protection from *her*. Lost in a haze of bloodlust, she sliced and diced each and every warrior, and they couldn't fight back; they remained unmoving.

Before Sabin tackled her, all ten warriors had been slain.

A vile curse erupted from Galen. What she'd just done...

Soon, other Sent Ones would sense the deaths and come for her. And because she was demon-possessed, the demon assassins had an added excuse to execute her.

A worry for another day.

He scanned the temple. Only one soldier remained standing. Gwen used the man's thigh as a step-stool, threw her free leg around his shoulders and used the momentum to pull herself into a sitting position. Balanced atop him, she placed her hands on different sides of his jaw and yanked, snapping his neck. He collapsed and she landed on her feet, walking away without a hitch in her step.

"Enough!" Leila tangled her fingers in Cronus's hair and straightened, dangling the head at her side. Panting, triumphant, she held up the second head, calling, "This is what happens to you when you mess with me and mine. Understand?"

"That's an awesome speech and all," Gwen said, "but, uh, the soldiers are dead now, so your audience is nonexistent. Sorry not sorry!"

Galen sheathed his weapons and stalked to Leila. She dropped the head and stalked to him. Then they were running, crashing together midway. He twirled her around, and she laughed, delighting him. Such a musical sound. Magical, too.

"You did it," he praised. "You did it *well*."

"I did, didn't I?"

"I love my present, sugar. Severed heads are *so* the new black."

She chuckled, and it only delighted him more.

"I'm never letting you go, Leila," he told her. "I love you. I love you so much."

Hope brightened her features, and it had nothing to do with the demon. "You do? I mean, I knew you did, but it's nice to hear."

"I do." He gave her words similar to the ones she'd given him. "Before you, I had no life. Now, you *are* my life."

"I love you, too. So much." She squeezed him tight. "I want to be with you, nothing held back. I want to be your partner in every way, shape, and form. And I want you and Aeron to be best friends forever. And I want you and Gwen to get along. You love her. Tell her! And I want Fox to admit that I'm perfect for you, and I also want her to call me Stepmother from now on."

A laugh escaped him, only to fade. He'd failed Gwen every day of her life, and today he'd failed Fox, allowing her to provoke the Sent Ones to war.

"For you, sugar? Anything." He set Leila on her feet and faced the others, who'd gathered around.

He'd tried to talk to Gwen a few times, yes, but he could have done more. Should have done more. In the end, he'd probably only hurt her worse, letting her think she meant little to him. After all, the harder you fought for something, the more you proved its worth to you.

He knew why. He'd feared rejection. But rejection was a dagger through the heart while regret was a dagger through the soul. No more regret. No more taking the coward's road. What you wanted, you fought for. No excuses. If you were knocked down, you got back up. Look at Leila. She'd risen from the ashes of her past, stronger and tougher than ever, an unbeatable force of feminine fury.

"Gwen," he began, keeping his arm around his woman.

"Fine! You talked me into it," Gwen told him grudgingly. "I'll give you a chance."

So easily? "I...thank you." It was then, in that moment, that he realized a startling truth. Part of the Harpy had wanted a relationship with him, too. When he'd needed her most, she hadn't hesitated to aid him. "I won't let you down."

"You found the scrapbook," Leila said with a smile, resting her head on his shoulder. "Didn't you?"

Gwen nodded, tears gathering and spilling. "It was... whatever. No big deal."

Leila grinned, smug. "I *knew* you'd cave as soon as you saw those pages."

Aeron patted Galen's shoulder. "Good job today."

"Yeah. You, too." *No big deal*, he thought in a mimic of his daughter. Meanwhile, he reeled. Was this good fortune truly his?

A sense of contentment settled inside him, stretched, and got comfortable, moving in for good.

He held out his hand. Aeron hesitated a moment, only a moment, before accepting. They shook, and the feeling of contentment intensified.

"Fox," Galen said next. "The Sent Ones will come for you. They'll—"

"I know," she croaked. At least her eyes had returned to their normal color, and the lines had faded from her skin. "Something came over me. No matter how hard I tried, I couldn't stop myself. They—" She smashed her lips together. Tremors shook her. "The things I did..."

Leila rushed over to draw the girl into her arms. "Don't worry. We'll protect you. We won't let anything bad happen to you."

At first, Fox was stiff as a board, but it wasn't long before she melted against the other woman. "Thank you. By the way, I'm not calling you Stepmother. But, what do you think of maybe, possibly considering thinking about calling each other...*friend*?"

Excitement pulsed from Leila. "Yes! Agreed. We will think about considering thinking about this."

Galen shared a confused look with Aeron, William, and Sabin. Uh...what the what now?

"I was wrong about you," Fox continued, wiping her tears with the back of her hand. "You aren't a weak link."

Wait. Hold up. Fox had told Leila she was a weak link? A growl rumbled in his chest.

Leila returned to his side and pressed a finger against his lips. "Keep your mouth zipped, lover boy. The big girls are talking."

He playfully nipped at the finger, earning another laugh from her. She'd once told him she would never be the girl she used to be, but here, now, she was that girl times twenty, and he loved her even more for it.

"Maybe you two deserve each other," Aeron muttered.

Galen had to swallow a new laugh. Despite the hardships they had yet to face, life could not get any better than this, he decided.

* * * *

Legion cuddled against Galen's side. They'd showered, made love, and lounged in bed until his present arrived. She'd expected his expression to shine with happiness, and it had. But the strong, tough warrior had actually teared up. He'd hugged her, and kissed her, reverent.

"I knew I loved you," he'd said, awed, "knew I'd give my life for yours. But this joy...I've never known its like. Never knew it was a possibility for one such as me."

"The same joy resides in me."

"Nothing the demons say can ever taint this," he'd said then. "It's too strong."

Now, they were back in bed, his heart beating in super-sync with hers, his warm breath fanning the top of her head, his fingers tracing the ridges of her spine. Hope for a better tomorrow glowed inside her, more powerful than ever, and she was more confident it had nothing to do with his demon. For the first time in her existence, she was truly content.

"*I* have a present for *you*," he said.

"Me? Besides the endless orgasms?" She clapped. "Gimme!"

"In *addition to* all those orgasms." He kissed her ear, then leaned over and slid a box out from under the bed.

Legion ripped the pretty pink wrapping, tore off the lid, and stared down at the biggest, most beautiful tiara she'd ever seen, with diamond roses. For a moment, her eyes misted. She had no words.

"The pins double as a weapon," he said. "You are my queen, and you require appropriate adornments."

"Thank you!" She anchored the piece to her crown before pushing Galen to his back and straddling his waist. "I have a sudden urge to sit upon my throne."

Many sweaty hours later, they reclined in bed once again. Legion still wore the tiara. Living in hell, she'd been deprived of all things beautiful. Now, she had the most beautiful man, body and soul, and the most beautiful jewels. The most beautiful life.

Only one thing cast a pallor on their future.

"You were right. The Sent Ones will come for Fox," she said, cuddling closer to her man.

"Yes. We must prepare for another war."

Fate sure was a fickle wench, wasn't she? For Legion, the decision to go after Cronus had cemented a better future. For Fox, the decision had altered the course of her life entirely—for the worse. "I meant what I said. I will fight by your side, and I will do everything in my power to guard our friend." Fox was part of Legion's family now, and family mattered.

"Thank you, sugar."

"For you, lover boy, anything."

"I know that, and I owe you thanks for it, too. You, my perfect mate, have given me everything I've ever wanted, everything I've ever needed, and so much more."

"Galen," she said. "You're putting me up on a pedestal...and I like it. Never stop."

He snorted. "I put you on a pedestal so I can look up your skirt."

That's my man. "Tell me something." Looking at him beneath the fan of her lashes, she asked, "Was I worth the wait?"

Galen used his wings to lift their bodies and flip her over. He loomed over her, locks of pale hair tumbling over his forehead. His ocean blues glittered with euphoria. "Leila, you are worth *everything*."

The corners of her mouth slowly lifted as satisfaction saturated every cell in her body. "So are you, lover boy. So are you."

THE END

* * * *

Also from 1001 Dark Nights and Gena Showalter, discover The Darkest Assassin, coming December 10, 2019.

Sign up for the 1001 Dark Nights Newsletter
and be entered to win a Tiffany Key necklace.

There's a contest every month!

Go to www.1001DarkNights.com to subscribe.

As a bonus, all subscribers will receive a free copy of
Discovery Bundle Three
Featuring stories by
Sidney Bristol, Darcy Burke, T. Gephart
Stacey Kennedy, Adriana Locke
JB Salsbury, and Erika Wilde

Discover 1001 Dark Nights Collection Five

Go to www.1001DarkNights.com for more information.

WOUND TIGHT by Lorelei James
A Rough Riders/Blacktop Cowboys Novella®

STRONG by Kylie Scott
A Stage Dive Novella

DRAGON NIGHT by Donna Grant
A Dark Kings Novella

TEMPTING BROOKE by Kristen Proby
A Big Sky Novella

HAUNTED BE THE HOLIDAYS by Heather Graham
A Krewe of Hunters Novella

CONTROL by K. Bromberg
An Everyday Heroes Novella

HUNKY HEARTBREAKER by Kendall Ryan
A Whiskey Kisses Novella

THE DARKEST CAPTIVE by Gena Showalter
A Lords of the Underworld Novella

Discover 1001 Dark Nights Collection One

Go to www.1001DarkNights.com for more information.

FOREVER WICKED by Shayla Black
CRIMSON TWILIGHT by Heather Graham
CAPTURED IN SURRENDER by Liliana Hart
SILENT BITE: A SCANGUARDS WEDDING by Tina Folsom
DUNGEON GAMES by Lexi Blake
AZAGOTH by Larissa Ione
NEED YOU NOW by Lisa Renee Jones
SHOW ME, BABY by Cherise Sinclair
ROPED IN by Lorelei James
TEMPTED BY MIDNIGHT by Lara Adrian
THE FLAME by Christopher Rice
CARESS OF DARKNESS by Julie Kenner

Also from 1001 Dark Nights

TAME ME by J. Kenner

Discover 1001 Dark Nights Collection Two

Go to www.1001DarkNights.com for more information.

Discover 1001 Dark Nights Collection Three

Go to www.1001DarkNights.com for more information.

Discover 1001 Dark Nights Collection Four

Go to www.1001DarkNights.com for more information.

ROCK CHICK REAWAKENING by Kristen Ashley
ADORING INK by Carrie Ann Ryan
SWEET RIVALRY by K. Bromberg
SHADE'S LADY by Joanna Wylde
RAZR by Larissa Ione
ARRANGED by Lexi Blake
TANGLED by Rebecca Zanetti
HOLD ME by J. Kenner
SOMEHOW, SOME WAY by Jennifer Probst
TOO CLOSE TO CALL by Tessa Bailey
HUNTED by Elisabeth Naughton
EYES ON YOU by Laura Kaye
BLADE by Alexandra Ivy/Laura Wright
DRAGON BURN by Donna Grant
TRIPPED OUT by Lorelei James
STUD FINDER by Lauren Blakely
MIDNIGHT UNLEASHED by Lara Adrian
HALLOW BE THE HAUNT by Heather Graham
DIRTY FILTHY FIX by Laurelin Paige
THE BED MATE by Kendall Ryan
PRINCE ROMAN by CD Reiss
NO RESERVATIONS by Kristen Proby
DAWN OF SURRENDER by Liliana Hart

Also from 1001 Dark Nights

Tempt Me by J. Kenner

About Gena Showalter

Gena Showalter is the *New York Times* and *USA TODAY* bestselling author of the spellbinding Lords of the Underworld, Otherworld Assassins, and Gods of War series, as well as three young adult series—The Forest of Good and Evil, Everlife and the White Rabbit Chronicles--and the highly addictive Original Heartbreakers series.

In addition to being a National Reader's Choice and two time RITA nominee, her romance novels have appeared in Cosmopolitan (Red Hot Read) and Seventeen magazine. She was interviewed on Nightline and has been mentioned in Orange is the New Black. Her books have been translated in multiple languages.

She's hard at work on her next novel, a tale featuring an alpha male with a dark side and the strong woman who brings him to his knees. Check her website often to learn more about Gena, her menagerie of rescue dogs, and all her upcoming books. https://genashowalter.com

The Darkest Assassin
A Lords Of The Underworld Novella
By Gena Showalter
Coming December 10, 2019

Fox is a demon-possessed immortal with many talents.
--Ability to open portals—check
--Power to kill the most dangerous Sent Ones—check
--Scare away any man who might want to date her—mate
Now, the keeper of Distrust has been marked for death, a winged assassin with rainbow-colored eyes tracking her every move, determined to avenge the males she accidentally decimated. If only she could control the desire to rip off his clothes…

Bjorn is a fierce warrior with many complications.
--Tragic, torture-filled past—check
--A wife he was forced to wed, who is draining his life force—check
--Ever-intensifying desire for the enigmatic Fox—mate
Never has he hesitated to exterminate an evil being. Until now. The sharp-tongued female with a shockingly vulnerable heart tempts him in ways no one else ever has, threatening his iron control.

But, as Fate itself seems to conspire against the unlikely pair, both old and new enemies emerge. And Fox and Bjorn must fight to survive.

And learn to love…

The Darkest Warrior
Lords of the Underworld
By Gena Showalter

A searing Lords of the Underworld tale by *New York Times* bestselling author Gena Showalter, featuring a beastly prince and the wife he will wage war to keep

He is ice...

Puck the Undefeated, host of the demon of Indifference, cannot experience emotion without punishment, so he allows himself to feel nothing. Until *her*. According to ancient prophecy, she is the key to avenging his past, saving his realm and ruling as king. All he must do? Steal her from the man she loves—and marry her.

She is fire...

Gillian Shaw has suffered many tragedies in her too-short life, but nothing could have prepared the fragile human for her transition into immortality. To survive, she must wed a horned monster who both intrigues and frightens her...and become the warrior queen she was born to be.

Together they burn.

As a rising sense of possession and obsession overtake Puck, so does insatiable lust. The more he learns about his clever, resourceful wife, the more he craves her. And the more time Gillian spends with her protective husband, the more she aches for him. But the prophecy also predicts an unhappily-ever-after. Can Puck defeat fate itself to keep the woman who brought his deadened heart back to life? Or will they succumb to destiny, losing each other...and everything they've been fighting for?

* * * *

A bomb of fury discharged inside Gillian, leaving a trail of devastation in its wake. Her heart melted against her ribs, warping the beat, and the sides of her lungs fused together.

Red dots flickered through her sight line, giving her tunnel vision. *Must destroy Puck!*

Launching onto his back, she hammered her fists into his chest. With each blow, sharp pains consumed *her* chest. Who cared? What was pain?

"Coward! Liar!" The worst insult of them all. "You disgust me." Not good enough. "You *repulse* me." Better.

"You are alive because of me."

"I'm miserable because of you!"

Regret seemed to pulse from him, there and gone in a flash. An illusion? Too late to tell. With a screech, she switched her aim to his face, and battered his nose. More pain, blood pouring down her mouth and chin. Still she didn't care.

Puck caught her wrists in a bruising grip, effectively ending her tirade. "My news should thrill you. After I drop you off with my friends, I'll return to the mortal realm to recruit William. He'll help me win back my crown, and I'll sever my bond to you."

Deep breath in, deep breath out. *Tamp down your fury. Act as if all is well. When the time comes, strike.*

First, she had to gather information. "What do you mean, you'll sever our bond?" she asked through clenched teeth. "We can officially divorce without dying?"

"That is the plan, aye." He offered no more, just resumed marching forward.

Um, did he not realize plans could be derailed? "Explain," she insisted, trying to hop off his back.

Silent, he readjusted her position and tightened his grip, ensuring every step rubbed her breasts against him. Lance after lance of pleasure tore through her, and she hissed.

"Let me down. Now. I won't fight you anymore." Not yet, anyway.

Perhaps the fear in her voice spurred him on. He wrapped an arm around her waist and swung her around. For a split second, she hung upside down. Then he righted her and placed her on her feet, directly in front of him.

"I will do *anything* to win my crown," he told her. "No deed is too dark. No task too gruesome."

The fire in her veins cooled. "Why?"

"Long ago, my brother betrayed me. He turned a champion into a monster and later killed our father, all to keep the Connacht crown for himself. He is destroying my home, hurting my people, and he must be stopped. I will save the lands and the clans, and I will avenge the wrongs done to me. According to the Oracles, my only hope of success was finding William of the Dark and wedding his woman."

Oracles? And oh, how casually he spoke of Gillian's doom.

"I *deserve* to wear the crown," he added. "I deserve vengeance. And I will be good to my people. I just need William's help."

"You're despicable," she spat.

"I know. But at least you're still alive. I saved you from certain death, something your precious William *wasn't* willing to do."

"Thanks for the reminder, goat man. But to what end?" she snapped. "Sometimes death is preferable to life." Her stephorrors had taught her that lesson very well. "William is smart. He'll know better than to trust you."

Puck hiked his wide shoulders in a shrug—a *shrug!*—and offered no assurances to the contrary.

She had to escape him, had to warn William.

Gillian faked left and darted right, but only made it four steps away before Puck caught her.

"Brace yourself," he said. "We enter my homeland in five, four, three, two..."

She attempted to wrench free, but he tightened his hold.

Between one blink and the next, everything changed. The humid heat of the rain forest morphed into cold desert winds, grains of sand pelting her skin. The drop in temperature shocked her system and momentarily rendered her immobile.

Two golden suns shone from a purple-red sky. There were no homes that she could see. No animals, bodies of water or people.

Escape. Now! She spun, shoved Puck out of the way and soared through the invisible doorway they'd just exited—

Nope. She ate sand.

"Where is the doorway?" she screeched. Where had it gone? Puck peered up at the odd-colored sky, his arms spread, his legs braced apart. Before her eyes, he transformed, the horns vanishing, and the fur on his legs quickly following suit. His cheekbones, once sharp enough to cut glass, softened some- what. His claws retracted, and the boots and hooves turned to mist, revealing human feet.

Not just beautiful. Utterly exquisite... But also a stranger to her.

She'd rather deal with the devil she knew.

He closed his eyes, inhaled...exhaled...as if savoring the moment. Another deception, surely. This horrible male savored nothing.

"How is this possible?" she demanded.

"A right of birth and magic. But it hasn't happened in so long... I thought the ability gone forever."

No way, no how magic controlled his appearance. Absolutely impossible! Except, he'd just gone from beast to chic in less than a blink. Denial was silly. Magic truly existed, and not just the hocus-pocus variety.

One day, too many fantastical things would happen and her mind would break.

On behalf of 1001 Dark Nights,

Liz Berry and M.J. Rose would like to thank ~

Steve Berry

Doug Scofield

Kim Guidroz

Jillian Stein

InkSlinger PR

Dan Slater

Asha Hossain

Chris Graham

Fedora Chen

Kasi Alexander

Jessica Johns

Dylan Stockton

Richard Blake

and Simon Lipskar

34990422R00104

Made in the USA
Middletown, DE
31 January 2019